Bloodline

By
Chris Wright

Providing Quality, Professional
Author Services
www.bookmanmarketing.com

ISBN: 1-59453-544-2

Previous Works By Chris Wright

Rockabye Baby

Heartstopper

Operation Overflow
(The Amazing Adventure of Dash Fordham vs. Dr, Gums)

Trouble in Turn Four

For Megan,
My Wife,
My Love,
My Life.

*   *   *

"It takes a whole village to raise a child," is an often used ancient African proverb, recently popularized by Hillary Clinton. The old adage correctly infers that the success of one individual is often the result of the combined efforts of many others. In this case truer words have never been spoken as once again a village of experiences, opinions and insights have enabled me to finish my fifth book.

To Rich Pegram, Jacques Natz and the entire WTHR family thank for your understanding and support of this project. Specifically I must thank John Stehr for sharing his intricate knowledge of conventions and the whole political process, and to Carolyn Williams thank you for your invaluable contribution to the final draft of the manuscript.

To Judy Sprenglemeyer thanks for saving the day when my computer crashed. Your only hard copy of the manuscript kept the project alive. To Robin Waldron thanks for offering your expertise and to Sheila Samson, the world's greatest story editor, thanks again, I could not have done this without you.

Most importantly to Carl Lau and the staff of Bookman Publishing, my deepest gratitude for giving me an outlet for my work.

Prologue

With heavy legs and numb feet the doctor slowly trudged down the starkly lit hallway. Bone weary from a long day's work he flexed his aching hands and stretched his arms as he walked. The harsh fluorescent light bouncing off the pristine walls and the well-worn but freshly waxed black and white floor made him squint - that and the fact that he had spent the last six hours in the O.R. fighting a battle against death. A battle the evil bastard was fiercely waging again. Nothing in medical school prepared any physician, especially this one, to deliver the blow he was about to hand out.

"I'm sorry," the medical man said as he slumped in his chair, "but we've done all we can do."

1

The soft orange glow bounced off the Manhattan skyline and poured through the window and the lush sound of Anita Baker crooning about her "Sweet Love" suffused the room. Olivia Cavillian Sagamore removed the black satin sleeping mask from her eyes and rolled over on her side to cast a baleful glare at the small digital clock radio sitting on the baroque antique dresser, summoning her to rise. She lay still for a minute more before she moved.

"Come on, old girl," she said as she slowly dragged herself from the bed. "Time to get moving."

Walking into the bathroom she turned water on, first in the shower then the sink. The plumbing in the historic building was antiquated and it took a while for the water to warm. Minutes later, with steam filling the room, she quickly brushed her teeth and tongue and stepped into the piping flow. With hot water pulsating on her back and drenching her body, she stood slumped against the damp wall. A million thoughts raced across her mind as she reached for the lilac soap she always used.

Fifteen minutes later, fully awakened by her morning shower, with one towel wrapped around her wet hair and another around her body, she began preparing for the meeting that would shift her life's direction. Standing in the walk-in closet that had once been a fourth bedroom, she chose an antique-white lace Anne Klein blouse and a three-piece navy blue Elle Tahari suit she'd purchased on one of her many trips to Saks Fifth Avenue. Rummaging through the drawers of her dresser, Olivia fished out her half-slip as she sang along with the clock radio as Barbra Streisand now hummed

1

softly in the background. The song ended and a traffic report gave the usual dose of bad news.

"The Triborough Bridge is congested due to an accident and there are minor delays on the Williamsburg Bridge and the Manhattan. On the Jersey side, smooth going through the tunnels, and the George Washington is showing an average flow for this hour. I'm Max Burns, Metro Traffic Watch."

"Thank goodness I don't have to deal with that madness this morning," she murmured with a sigh of relief as she sat on the side of the bed, slid her feet inside her panty hose, and drew them up her legs.

Although she still owned the grand Westchester County estate that had been in her family for three generations, she preferred to live in the city. Her three-bedroom Upper East Side apartment gave her more than enough space; and living in the city, close to her office and to the theatre, made life easier for her after her husband died.

Parker James Sagamore of the upstate New York Sagamores, had been by her side since her college days. After a brief courtship the two married after her senior year. Their daughter Jessica was born less than a year after. Although the union between the two was less than ideal in many ways, it was very functional and extremely profitable. The marriage cemented the financial bond between two of New York state's wealthiest families. While the Cavillians were firmly entrenched in the northeast's finest social circles, it was the Sagamores who brought the larger fortune to the union.

Settling into the eighteen-room mansion built by Wilson Cavillian, Olivia's grandfather, the young Sagamore newlyweds were the toast of the town. Always careful to project a positive public image, the two were viewed by many East Coast socialites as the perfect couple; but as

Sagamore Investments International grew more successful, their social demands increased and so did the void dividing them. Parker quickly grew tired of the social burden and more often than not had to be forced to paint on the public facade that once came naturally. On the other hand Olivia thrived in the spotlight. Whether it was an evening at the Met, a fund-raising gala, the latest Broadway opening or a simple dinner party, she sparkled.

As a Cavillian, Olivia had always known a public life filled with one must-attend event after another, but her husband was from the opposite end of the social spectrum. The Sagamore wealth had come from a working-class heritage. Parker's parents had spent long hours behind the counters of the eleven jewelry stores the family operated with a fair-value-at-a-fair-price mentality. They placed little value on socializing so Parker never developed those networking abilities.

Despite his minimal social skills, his business acumen was high. Parker had been well schooled at negotiating international business deals from his youthful days of buying and transporting diamonds from Amsterdam and South Africa to the various stores in the tri-state area. A shrewd businessman with a knack for developing companies, he started an investment firm. His knowledge of world trading policies and his tireless work ethic, coupled with Olivia's connections and knowledge of domestic finance, destined Sagamore Investments International for success.

Over their three decades of working side by side, the pair grew the company initially funded by his family's money into a multi-million-dollar business. Although Olivia had been an integral part of the company's success, it had been Parker's vision more than hers. Now, four years after his death, she stood ready to sell the business and move on to a new chapter in her life.

Olivia dried and curled her hair. Once shoulder-length and golden blonde it was now tinged with gray and much shorter than before. Always one to wear as little makeup as possible she lined her eyebrows and dabbed on a touch of blush. Then she added lipstick before closing the clasps on the Rolex watch that had been one of the last gifts from her late husband.

The weather forecaster on the morning news had predicted an unseasonably cool morning with a possible record low so Olivia slipped on a light-weight trench coat. The lock clicked behind her as she walked out the door. Her long graceful legs glided across the carpeted hallway and she pushed the elevator button. She scrutinized her five-foot eight-inch reflection on the mirrored wall of the elevator car and realized that she forgot to put on her earrings.

"I'd forget my head if it wasn't planted on," she grumbled as she turned and unlocked the door to go back inside.

She retrieved the one-carat diamond earrings she always wore and took the elevator from her fourth-floor apartment to the lobby, slipping her well-manicured fingers into a pair of black Isotoner gloves as the elevator descended.

"Good morning, Carl," Olivia said to the doorman as he held the door open for her.

"Morning to you, Mrs. Sagamore. May I get you a taxi?" he asked, knowing she would say no, as she most often did.

"No, thank you, Carl. I think I'll walk today," she said before stepping out into the unusually cool August morning air.

"Yes ma'am. You have a good day."

"You do the same," she said as she walked toward her office.

Unless it was raining or snowing, Olivia preferred to walk the six blocks to Sagamore Investments International, which was on the ninth floor of the Echelon Building on Seventh Avenue. She made her usual stops at the newsstand on the corner at Fifth Avenue to get a copy of the New York Times, and at Starbucks for a cappuccino and a bagel, before heading to her office. She loved the hustle and bustle of the city, and walking to work breathing in fresh air invigorated her.

Today she walked more deliberately, knowing this was a walk she would not be making much longer. Frazier Whitley had been offering to buy the business since Parker died, but she had resisted. However, now that Jessica was about to deliver Olivia's first grandchild, her priorities had changed. She realized she'd rather spend more time being a doting grandmother and less time negotiating deals, making investments and worrying about the European bond market.

"Good morning, Mrs. Sagamore," the young secretary said from behind her desk as Olivia walked in.

"Good morning, Carol. Are you getting any sleep yet?" Olivia asked. The woman, almost the same age as Jessica, had recently returned from a maternity leave.

"A little," she said. "Tammy only sleeps about four hours at a time, and then it's time for a feeding."

"Hang in there, she'll let you get a full night's rest in a few months."

"Soon you'll be in the same boat with me. How is Jessica?"

"She's fine. Just three more months to go and I'll be a granny."

"You'll be the best!" Carol said with a beaming smile.

"Thanks," Olivia said as she sorted through a stack of messages. "It's been so long since I was around a baby."

"It's like riding a bike. You never forget how to do it."

"I hope you're right, Carol, I hope you're right," Olivia said as she walked down the hall to her office to wait for her next appointment.

It was a meeting Olivia anticipated with mixed emotions. While she knew that the time was right, Parker would never have approved of her selling "his" business. He always considered it his, even though she had put in equal sweat equity. It was the business that had supported them, divided them, and eventually killed him at the age of sixty-two.

A routine checkup two years before he died detected prostate cancer, but he'd kept the test results secret. He delayed starting treatment until he returned, first from a trip to Tokyo, then a long, drawn-out negotiation in Lisbon, then a trek to Australia. A year after he was diagnosed he began treatment, but it was too late. By then the disease had spread to his spine and lungs, and despite aggressive treatment, he was dead less than a year later.

Sitting at her desk, Olivia decided to write a letter explaining the sale of Sagamore Investments International to Whitley Worldwide. Were this an ordinary memo she would have dictated it to her secretary but she and Frazier had taken great care to prevent the deal from being leaked in order to avoid panic among clients and employees of both companies. Carefully choosing her words, she turned on her computer and began to type.

To the valued clients and treasured employees of Sagamore Investments International:

It is with great joy and anticipation that I announce the sale of Sagamore Investments International to Whitley

Worldwide. I know that this may come as a surprise to many of you, but since the death of my husband Parker four years ago, I have had many offers to sell the business, and from time to time, entertained the notion of doing so. I refrained, as I never felt the time was right for either myself or the company. Recently, Frazier Whitley, a long time family friend and well-respected entrepreneur, approached me about a buyout. Knowing my clients and employees would be in safe hands, I decided that he would be the best person to continue what Parker and I started.

As most of you know, I am about to become a grandmother for the first time, and that combined with Frazier's generous offer - makes this a perfect time to move on.

On a personal note, I have a few things to say.

To my associates, please know that Frazier has given me every assurance that there will be no changes in personnel related to his taking over.

To my clients, I'm sure all of you know of Frazier and his reputation and that you will be in excellent hands.

Please join me in welcoming Frazier Whitley in his efforts to continue our commitment to excellence as I venture off into the next chapter of my life.

Olivia Sagamore

"Mrs. Sagamore, Mr. Whitley is here to see you," the secretary's voice said through the intercom as Olivia typed her last few words and printed the document.

"Carol, show them to the conference room and make them comfortable."

"Yes, ma'am."

She summoned her attorney, Harry Fields. "Harry, you can come on down. Frazier's here," she said.

"Olivia, are you sure you want to do this?" her longtime confidante asked.

"Yes, I'm sure. You can meet us in the conference room."

Promptly at 9:30 a.m. Olivia walked into the room. Frazier Whitley was already seated, flanked by two attorneys adorned in almost identical dark blue suits with the requisite power ties. The moment she entered the room, they all rose and Frazier walked over to her.

Olivia, how are you on this lovely day?" Frazier began.

"I'm fine."

"Olivia, we go way back, so I won't beat around the bush. I've coveted this business for years, but I have to ask..."

"Yes, Frazier, I'm sure I want to do this. I wouldn't sell to anyone but you, and I'm going to do it today."

"Let's do business," he said briskly as he pointed to the conference table with a graceful flourish.

"Let's," she said as she walked to her customary seat at the head of the table.

"Good morning, everyone," Harry Fields said as he entered the room.

After briefly exchanging pleasantries with Frazier's legal eagles, Harry was all business. He took his seat next to Olivia and the exchange of paperwork began. More than two hours later a stack of documents outlining the change of ownership, personnel assignments, client-agency agreements and bank drafts were signed and exchanged across the table. To the untrained eye it looked like a maze of legalese, but to Frazier and Olivia it marked the conclusion of one regime and the dawn of another. By the end of the meeting Frazier Whitley was owner of Sagamore Investments International, and the now-retired Olivia Sagamore was seven million dollars richer.

2

A large platform adorned in red, white and blue bunting sat in the shadows of majestic, snow-capped, mountain peaks. The day was warm and only a few wispy cirrus clouds streaked the sky. With the clear blue water of Barr Lake and the lush greenery of the state park behind the stage, the setting was almost too picturesque for the political rally. The highlight of the event was the guest speaker, California Governor Jeff Burris. Over four thousand people had gathered for the five-hundred-dollar-a-plate picnic lunch and his words had swept the adoring crowd into a frenzy.

"President Greenlee has turned his back on those who worked so hard to elect him. There are some clear differences in our positions on the issues, so let me draw a distinct line between us. Let me say, in closing, that I will address the air quality concerns of the Front Range Coalition; that I vow to continue efforts to protect the Rocky Mountains from strip mining, and that I will never, ever, allow oil exploration within the Colorado National Forest. I have to leave now, but I want to thank you, each and every one of you, for your warm western hospitality. Thank you, and God bless!" The governor ended the speech with a vibrant wave.

U.S. presidential candidate Jeff Burris was hot on the campaign trail. After the fund-raiser in Denver, where he collected more than two million dollars, he was on a plane to Indianapolis. As president of the National Association of Governors, he was scheduled to give the keynote speech at dinner. The NAG meeting was nothing more than a glorified photo opportunity, since the organization was expected to back his candidacy. Nevertheless, the endorsement would be worth a few points in the polls, and that would help on the East Coast where he trailed the incumbent.

More important than the dinner speech or the endorsement was a planned meeting with fellow governors and party leaders to discuss the vice presidential nominee. Jeff had his own idea for a running mate, but in this case he would have to defer to the party. When he first decided to run for president, Jeff thought he'd have more autonomy; but he now realized he was nothing more than a puppet of his party.

Burris had smoothly made the sizeable transition from small-town attorney to governor but he knew his political pockets were more than a few chips shy in this high-stakes political game. A steady march through the spring primaries that culminated in a strong showing on Super Tuesday had garnered him the delegates necessary for nomination. His victories over four senators, two congressmen and two governors solidified his status as the party standard bearer but still he knew he lacked the clout to push his own agenda.

Burris arrived in Indianapolis and gave the speech that was written for him. For the nominating convention he wrote his own words, but in most cases he delegated speech writing to his staff. He posed for pictures and for the news cameras after the endorsement was announced by Roderick Schilling, chairman of the Constitution Party. When the public display was finished the power brokers gathered for a powwow.

Before going into the meeting Jeff pulled his campaign manager aside and gave him instructions:

"Tim, when we get inside don't say a word. Schilling is going to ramrod this thing down my throat and there is nothing I can do about that. Make a transcript of everything that is said so we can find out who's on our side and who's not. Once I'm elected I'll bury all of my enemies, one by one, starting with Schilling."

"Do you really think they've already selected a vice-presidential candidate?"

"They handpicked me, didn't they?" Burris deadpanned.

Inside the conference room at the Marriott were three of the most powerful men in the nation, men who worked behind closed doors to shape the policies and make the decisions that ruled the lives of millions. Two of the three had accepted Jeff Burris' candidacy only as a compromise in order to unseat the incumbent. Sitting around the table sipping coffee and swilling scotch were Roderick Schilling, governor of Minnesota; Petey Burkett, governor of Texas; and Arthur McClain, governor of Pennsylvania.

"Jeff, you're doing a great job on the campaign trail. Greenlee's people are shaking in their boots, there's no wonder why he won't come out of the Rose Garden and debate you," the Pennsylvania governor said, giving Jeff a warm handshake.

"Arty, you've shown a lot of confidence in me. I thank you for your help and for your friendship," he answered.

"Jeff, pour yourself a drink, and we'll get started," the party chairman said, tapping Jeff on the shoulder as he walked by.

"Thanks, Roderick, I'll just have a cup of coffee."

"Yeah, let's get this love-in over, and get down to business," said the cantankerous governor of Texas.

"I just want everyone to know that I'm completely open to suggestions about a running mate, but ultimately it's my decision," Jeff Burris said as the meeting started.

"That's what you think," Petey Burkett snorted as he drained his glass and refilled it as quickly.

"Thanks for being open-minded Jeff, but we need to balance the ticket if we stand any chance of winning," said Roderick Schilling.

"And that's exactly why I think we should go with Ward Cargellon out of Florida," Jeff answered. "He's moderate, he'll appeal to the Deep South and the East Coast, and he's experienced."

"You've done your homework, and ordinarily he'd make a good choice. But he's locked in a budget battle in his own state. In two years Florida is going to have to implement a state income tax to stay afloat, and that won't win him any friends. Politically he's already dead, he just doesn't know it yet."

"Not enough tax money coming from all those retirees," the Texas governor chimed in through his tobacco-stained teeth.

"That, and the fact that his administration squandered a one hundred thirty-four million dollar surplus," Roderick Schilling added.

Jeff knew that a running mate had been chosen. He also knew that it was someone he wouldn't approve of. He took a deep breath before posing his next question and braced himself for the answer. When they told him who it was, he was shocked beyond belief.

"Do you have anyone particular in mind?" Jeff asked tenatively.

"Eddie Blanton, from Ohio."

"'Touchdown' Eddie Blanton! You've got to be kidding?" he said, fighting to hold back any further outbursts.

"Look, Jeff, this guy is a well-known football hero. He made the Hall of Fame on the first ballot. Politically he's paid his dues as a three-term mayor of Columbus, Ohio, and now he's in his second term in the U.S. Senate. He's originally from New York, so he has a Midwest and an East Coast connection. With his high popularity from his gridiron days, we're lucky he's not running against us," Arthur McClain said.

As hard as he tried, Jeff couldn't contain another outburst.

"The last thing I need is some pretty-boy football player to help me get elected. I got this far on my own and I can get to the White House the same way!"

"Get real Jeff! You're in deep trouble and you know it!" Roderick Schilling shot back. "You're at least fifty million dollars short of what you need to get elected, and to get your hands on a big chunk of old East Coast money you need a link, and we all know you don't have it."

"I was born in Philadelphia, and the last time I checked it was on the East Coast!" Jeff Burris retorted.

"You haven't lived in Pennsylvania since you were three years old, everyone knows that!" Roderick said.

"I've spent lots of time back East visiting friends and family on holidays and vacations," he pleaded.

"Drop it, Jeff. Whether you like it or not, Blanton is on the ticket!" Roderick thundered. "I want it done right, so I'm making the nomination speech myself."

Roderick Schilling was the most powerful man in the Constitution Party. If it weren't for the fact that he was sixty-seven years old and had a heart that could fail any day now, he'd be on the ticket himself. Having made two unsuccessful attempts at the presidency he was damaged goods, but he still had enough clout to decide whom the party would run. Roderick had viewed Jeff Burris as a weak candidate from the start and had pushed the Constitution Party to put its power behind Eddie Blanton, but some party leaders felt

Eddie needed more time on the national stage, so they compromised on the better-known governor of California.

"Plus, down in my neck of the woods you're viewed as just another right-wing, smooth-talking, over-tanned, California golden boy," drawled Texas governor Petey Burkett.

"So what do they think about Blanton, down in your neck of the woods?" Jeff bristled.

"They think he's a winner! Hell, he beat Houston for one of them football championships!" Petey answered, his speech slurred from his fourth drink of the night.

"We need a liberal on the ticket, Jeff, and his being a football hero doesn't hurt," Arthur McClain said.

"I understand that, but I thought we'd balance the ticket with someone more seasoned," Jeff answered.

"If we wanted someone more seasoned, I'd be running, not you," Roderick Schilling added.

Jeff thought what he dared not say: "You've already blown two opportunities to get to the White House. Eight years ago you lost by a landslide and four years ago Anthony Greenlee beat you in your own home state. If you were running now, you'd be so far be behind it would be a joke."

Knowing when to concede defeat, he wisely kept his private thoughts private. He was confident he'd be around long enough to put the final nail in the coffin of Schilling's political career, and he knew that day would come soon, since Schilling was up for re-election in two years. Savoring the thought of sweet revenge, Jeff Burris fought the urge to smile as he slowly sipped from his cup.

"Any dirt on him?" Jeff asked as he glanced at his campaign manager, who was unobtrusively taking notes. "You know how much I hate surprises."

"We've already checked him out. He's been married for almost thirty years. He has a son in medical school, no grandkids, and he's squeaky clean," Roderick Schilling added.

"Think he'll accept the VP nod?" the nominee asked.

"Hell yeah, he'll accept the nod. Who doesn't want to sit a heartbeat away from the Oval Office?" the Texas governor added.

Always the voice of reason in tempestuous situations, Arthur McClain walked across the room and calmly put a hand on Jeff's shoulder. "Jeff, we don't have any doubts about you, but a team is only as strong as its bench. We really believe we need this guy on board otherwise we wouldn't force him on you."

"As long as he understands who the number-one quarterback is on this team," Jeff said.

3

Freshly trimmed shrubs and palm trees lined the cleanly swept streets of Florida's largest city. Even mosquitoes, know to swarm in the late summer steambath, were on their best behavior as the area hosted the largest political gathering in its history. The event, which came after two years of meticulous planning, served to anoint south Florida's multi-ethnic population as the model of the new melting pot of American voters.

"The city of Miami and the entire state of Florida welcomes the Constitution Party National Convention!" Mayor Carlos Fuentes boomed into the microphone.

The first two nights had been a rousing success highlighted by the dramatic roll call of the states and for the third night in a row the Dade County Convention Center was packed to the rafters with a sea of red, white and blue. Delegates from all across the nation applauded and cheered as balloons rained from the ceiling and confetti filled the air. It was a festive night that party leaders and followers hoped would launch their candidate, California Governor Jeff Burris, to the presidency of the United States.

"Voters across America have spoken clearly, and tonight we are here to carry out their mandate. We are here to celebrate the nomination of a great man, the man who will lead us through the fall campaign, the man who will lead us to the White House, the man who will lead this great nation for the next four years," Mayor Fuentes said.

As planned, his speech was interrupted several times by the exuberant crowd. The interruptions were more for the benefit of the television audience across the nation. A united front had to be presented in order to attract undecided voters and to show party unity, a lack of which had cost the Constitution Party the last election.

"In order to lead the greatest nation on the planet a strong running mate is needed. To give the nomination speech for the vice-presidential nominee is a great man in his own right. To say he's the Chairman of the Constitution Party is not to do him justice. He's the heart, soul and conscience of the Constitution Party. Ladies, gentlemen and delegates, here's the Honorable Governor of the great state of Minnesota, Roderick Schilling."

The applause roared for the party's presidential nominee from the past two conventions as he took the podium. Schilling's function was not only to introduce the vice-presidential nominee, but also to pass the torch to the next party standard-bearer. No one in the audience had a doubt as to who the vice-presidential candidate would be.

Blanton was a popular choice, especially in the Midwest. His gridiron heroics had led Ohio State to its seventh national championship thirty years earlier. After a stellar collegiate career, he played professional football in Cleveland, leading the team to two world championships before retiring and going into politics.

"My fellow Americans, my duty here tonight is to nominate Senator Edward Keith Blanton for vice president of the United States," Roderick Schilling began as a deafening roar filled the arena. "On news programs coast to coast there has been a lot of talk about Jeff Burris and his choice for a running mate. The man who will work beside him as we usher in a new era of American ingenuity is not a Washington insider and he's not a political retread. He's an unconventional choice with unconventional ideas, for these oh-so-unconventional times."

The Minnesota governor continued his speech, extolling the virtues of the nominee and saluting his accomplishments. Ten minutes later he gave the crowd what they hungered for.

"Ladies and gentlemen, delegates, I present to you the Constitution Party vice-presidential nominee - from the great state of Ohio, 'Touchdown' Eddie Blanton!" Roderick Schilling announced as the crowd cheered.

The adoring crowd waved signs and suddenly the piped-in music was replaced by the brassy sound of "The Best Damn Band in the Land" as two hundred twenty-five members of The Ohio State University marching band filled the stage playing "Carmen Ohio," the school fight song.

The band continued playing as Eddie Blanton rose on a podium. The former quarterback-turned-politician took center stage and waved to his fans and delegates. The band finished its song and filed off the stage. "Eddie! Eddie! Eddie!" the crowd chanted as he posed for the cameras. He was used to performing before much larger crowds since his collegiate days, so this was nothing new to him. He waited until the applause subsided and then gave the thirty-minute speech Roderick Schilling had written for him.

On the fourth night of the convention came the moment the nation had waited for. Mayor Carlos Fuentes, who would soon announce his candidacy for governor of Florida, gave the speech that would bring him more fame and notoriety than his two terms as mayor of the state's largest city.

"Behind every great man there is a great woman. In front of every man there is a great woman, and beside every man is a great woman. Our nominee tonight is fortunate enough to have three great women who will nominate him for the highest office in the land. Ladies and gentleman, Constitution Party Delegates, I present to you the first lady of the great state of California, Elizabeth Randolph Burris, and her lovely daughters, Janice and Sharon!"

An explosion of confetti filled the room and the three women strolled to center stage as the adoring throng clapped wildly and cheered louder than before. Dressed in a sparkling dark green evening gown, Elizabeth, a former Miss California, still had her beauty-queen grace and beauty. She loved the spotlight as much as her husband, and she had raised their girls on the campaign trail.

They painted on their bright, wide campaign smiles they had used for years and waved enthusiastically to the crowd. Free of scandal or controversy, three-fourths of the Burris family prepared to propel the fourth member to the Oval Office as the strains of "I Love You, California" the state song, filled the convention center.

The excitement continued as the three Burris women walked to the edge of the stage to shake hands with their admirers. After making sure enough photos were taken, the two young women exited the stage. Elizabeth walked to the podium and proudly watched as they disappeared from her view and paused before giving the most important speech of her husband's career.

It had been his choice, against the advice of party leaders, for his wife to give his nomination speech. Although there were a couple of up-and-coming party members considered better suited for the job, Roderick Schilling relented and allowed Elizabeth to deliver the address - a speech he penned himself.

"Thank you, ladies and gentlemen, for your warm welcome, and thanks for your support through the primaries. It was a long, tough contest and Jeff and I couldn't have made it without you," Elizabeth Burris said when the applause subsided ten minutes later.

19

"Burris! Burris! Burris! Burris!" the adoring crowd chanted, interrupting her speech for the first of what would be many times.

"Now that the primaries have been settled, it's time to move on to the general election. Our opponents like to talk about family values and tax programs, but what have they done over the past four years for working-class folks?"

The crowd that before cheered wildly, now booed lustily, voicing their displeasure with the mention of their adversary, the incumbent President Anthony Greenlee. Elected four years prior by a slim margin in a race characterized by poor turnout, the President was largely viewed as a lame duck leader, especially in this room.

"Well, tonight I'm going to introduce you to someone who knows family values. He's a working-class man who helped raise two daughters. A man who took his tax refunds and put new tires on his wife's beat-up old Honda Civic and made extra deposits in his kids' college funds. A man who spent Saturday mornings watching his daughters play soccer and who spent those same afternoons shopping with his wife at Wal-Mart. A man who still, to this day, makes one hell of a macaroni casserole," she said as the convention center erupted in laughter.

Born in Philadelphia, Jeff Burris grew up in Modesto, California. He was a graduate of Sacramento State University with an undergraduate degree in Urban Planning and received his law degree from UCLA. He and Elizabeth married during his first year of law school, and like many young couples, the would-be lawyer and the second-grade teacher struggled financially as they built their careers. When their first daughter was born, Jeff stayed home with the child during the day and attended class at night.

After graduation he opened his own firm in his hometown, and in the two decades that he practiced law, Jeff Burris gained a reputation as an intense but fair litigator. It was the case of the *City of Modesto vs. the California Water Company* that brought him to the forefront of the state's legal community and made him a champion in the San Joaquin Valley.

The city sued the water company for price gouging and poor water filtration and treatment policies. Against a large battery of more experienced corporate attorneys in a case no one expected him to win, he prevailed. The class-action lawsuit brought lower rates and better service to Modesto, and California Water Company customers were refunded an average three hundred dollars each. Garnering a total settlement of four hundred-fifty million dollars, his thirty percent fee made him an instant millionaire. After being elected state attorney general, he improved the state's conviction rate by twenty-seven percent.

After one term as attorney general, he was tapped by the Constitution Party for their gubernatorial nod. Elected by a landslide to his first term, he ran for re-election four years later. Outdistancing his opponent by more than a million votes brought him national attention and eventually led him to the presidential nomination.

Now, on a steamy mid-August evening, he sat across the street from the convention in a south Florida hotel room and watched the girl he'd met on a blind date over thirty-five years ago, nominate him for the most powerful office in the land.

"When I first met Jeff he was like most law students, full of lofty goals and high ideals, but a little short on money. In fact, he still owes me for paying for our first date. We went to see Warren Beatty and Faye Dunaway in *Bonnie and*

Clyde and we ate dinner at Jack-in-the-Box. I fell in love with him on that night, and I knew I'd follow him anywhere. Through the years I've stood beside him on the campaign trail. He and I have had our ups and downs, and we've weathered more than a few storms. We've raised children and grandchildren and now, once again, I'm on the trail with him. I'm not a politician and I'm not one for making speeches, but I stand here before you tonight to nominate the man I'm sure is ready to lead this country. Ladies and gentleman, respected delegates, I hereby nominate California Governor Jefferson Randolph Burris for the Presidency of the United States of America."

A robust version of "Hail to the Chief" burst through the loudspeakers, and balloons and confetti littered the air once again. Flanked by her daughters, Elizabeth beamed brightly. While some wives may have dreaded this moment, she had eagerly looked forward to it since the day Jeff decided to run for attorney general. The thought of being first lady of the nation was something she'd always dreamed of, and now it was well within her grasp. Hand-in-hand with her daughters, she walked to edge of the stage, basking in the applause.

Ten minutes after the music began, the crowd had just started to settle down when Jeff Burris strode confidently into the convention center. With his two grandsons in his arms he walked onto the stage and joined the rest of his family. The adoring crowd cheered their hero as he stepped to the edge of the stage and shook hands with as many of them as he could. He was known for his calculated, almost plodding style of leadership, and his appearance delighted his followers. What only his closest advisers knew was that his unlikely choice to deliver his nomination speech and his casual appearance were all part of his carefully orchestrated plan.

After allowing the applause to continue for another ten minutes, giving the press a lengthy photo opportunity, Jeff Burris made eye contact with his campaign manager signaling that he was ready to begin, and the speech he'd spent the past two weeks polishing was loaded in the Teleprompter.

Over the din he said to his wife, "Here we go. You and the girls can wait for me in the skybox."

"Good luck, Jeff. I love you," she said before giving him a kiss and leading the rest of the Burris clan off the stage.

He walked up to the podium and took a deep breath, savoring the moment and preparing to give the most important speech of his political career. He had visualized this moment many times before but as he stood there he realized that it was much better than he had ever dreamed. He also realized that he wanted to be elected president more than he'd previously thought. He motioned for the crowd to quiet down and cleared his throat before speaking.

"Mr. Chairman, delegates, and my fellow Americans. I humbly accept your nomination. Thank you for this high honor. I'd also like to thank my wife for the past thirty years and for her warm, loving speech nominating me for the presidency. I'd also like to thank her for paying for our first date - and one of these days, when I get a steady, good-paying job, I'll pay you back Lizzie, I swear."

Just four sentences into his speech he had already been interrupted by applause six times. He was off to a rolling start, and he needed to be. The words he spoke over the next forty-five minutes would define his candidacy.

"As I stand before you tonight in a place where so many immigrants have risked their very lives to come in search of a new way of life, I think it is more than appropriate to establish a new tradition. So tonight not only do I humbly and gratefully accept your nomination; but I also plan to let you know exactly where this candidate stands on the issues. Like the mighty Gulf Stream that runs along the East Coast and crosses the great Atlantic, I will reach out to our allies and repair the vital relationships that the current administration has ignored."

Jeff Burris continued, outlining his campaign strategy and governing vision for the nation. His speech was received enthusiastically and was interrupted by applause more than sixty times before he finished. At the end of his speech the strains of "Happy Days Are Here Again" filled the room.

The music continued as Eddie Blanton rose on a podium at stage left and Jeff Burris rose on a podium at stage right. Earlier that day their campaign manager had placed a football under the podium, and Jeff Burris took the football and tossed it across the stage to Blanton. The two men signaled touchdown and the crowd went wild over the made-for-television moment.

"Governor Burris, first of all, thank you," Eddie Blanton said. I look forward to working alongside you."

"Is there anything else you'd like to say to the people?" Jeff asked.

"I'm not a man who makes long speeches, I'm a man of action," he said as he lofted a perfect spiral high into the convention center. "And now I'm going to go backstage and get to work on our game plan. Governor Burris, before I leave let me give you and the rest of the nation my word: I vow to do whatever it takes to make our team successful and lead us to victory in November!" With those words Eddie Blanton left the stage as planned, leaving Jeff Burris alone in the spotlight.

4

The warm mid-August sun sparkled and there was a touch of humidity in the air. A few puffy cumulus clouds floated seemingly just above the skyline, casting shadows on the faces of the Empire State and Chrysler buildings. Horns blared and tempers flared while traffic showed its usual Saturday afternoon congestion in the heart of the theatre district. Martini's featured New York's largest year-round outdoor patio café, and oblivious to the crowded chatter around them the mother and daughter munched on a couple of grilled chicken Caesar salads.

"Mom, you've spent your whole life working the business. Now…" Jessica began.

Trying to ward off the speech she knew was coming, Olivia Sagamore raised her hand in submission. "I know," she said.

"GET A LIFE!" they both said in unison, bursting into laughter.

The two women cackled until Jessica could barely breathe. The first-time expectant mother reached into her purse for a tissue. She dabbed at her eyes, then pulled out an envelope and handed it to her mother.

"Take this; it's from me, Brad, and the baby. We've already paid for it so you have to take it."

"Oh, you shouldn't have," Olivia said as she opened the envelope.

"It's something you need."

"Oh, my God! I can't take this, not right now," Olivia said as she stared at the ticket for a southern Caribbean cruise.

"Of course you can, Mom. The cruise is only for seven days. Besides, once the baby is born you won't have time for a vacation. I'm going to need you," Jessica said as she took her mother's hand.

"Maybe I could take some time to relax and do some reading, but I don't need to go to the Caribbean for that."

"Mom, retired people travel. They do all the things they never had time for while they were working. It's time for you to live a little."

"I'll think about it. Maybe I could use a little time away."

"Yeah and get yourself a man while you're at it," her daughter said. "I hear those cruise ships are crawling with eligible men. Remember that show, The Love Boat."

"Oh yeah, and I'm sure they are all looking for fifty-three-year-old women."

"Maybe. And maybe Stella can get her groove back while she's there," she said referring to the film the two of them had seen together on their monthly girls movie night.

"Girl, your mother should wash your mouth out with soap," said Olivia playfully.

"Mom, I'm serious. Dad's been gone for a while now and, frankly, you guys were not the picture of wedded bliss."

"I did my best to make sure you never saw how bad things really were."

"Well, now you have a second chance, a chance to find love and be happy. I want that so badly for you."

"I have love and happiness and I'll have someone new to share it with as soon as you have that baby."

"Mom, you know what I mean."

"Yes, but I don't know if I'm willing to try."

"When it's the right boy, you'll know," Jessica said using words Olivia had spoken to her many times over the years as she rebounded from one broken relationship after another.

"I hate it when you turn my own words against me."

"Hey, that's what daughters are for."

"Are you sure you'd be alright if I went away?"

"The baby is not due for nine weeks. I'm fine."

"Okay, if you say so."

"I say so."

Three days later, on August 20th, Olivia Sagamore boarded a plane for Miami. Six hours after leaving her Manhattan apartment, she climbed the ramp to *The Memphis*, a Circle Cruise Lines ocean liner bound for a week in paradise. The eight-story ship was the length of ten football fields and on board *The Memphis* boasted two casinos, a forty-store shopping mall, fitness center, bank, hair salon and a full medical center among its amenities. With a staff of three hundred, the ship was built for trans-Atlantic cruises with a passenger capacity of two thousand.

Olivia boarded the ship with a pang of guilt. A cruise was something she had always hoped to share with Parker, but deep inside she knew that he would never have taken the time away from work, not even to be with her. Parker preferred to be buried in a sea of paperwork and deals. Work was his sanctuary away from the stress of being home, away from being alone with his wife.

"Mrs. Sagamore, I'm Connie Traylor and I'll be your hostess this week. If there is anything you need, night or day, feel free to call me," the woman said as she handed Olivia her business card.

"Hello, Connie, nice to meet you."

"The ship stewards will bring your luggage to your stateroom. If you'll follow me, I'll show you where your suite is located."

After an elevator ride to the second deck Olivia was shown to her stateroom. It had a cozy sitting area complete with a television, a mini-fridge, and a wet bar. She had a coffeemaker in her full bathroom and a queen-sized bed in her bedroom.

"I thought this would be a lot smaller," Olivia remarked.

"Oh, no, at Circle Cruise Lines we believe everyone should travel in spacious comfort," Connie replied.

"Well this certainly looks comfortable."

"I'm glad you like it. Is there anything else you need, ma'am?"

"No thanks, I'm fine for now."

"Well, here's your on-board itinerary. Everything is strictly voluntary. The ship sails in thirty minutes. Cocktails are at six, and dinner is at seven."

Connie opened the door to leave as the ship stewards were bringing in Olivia's luggage. Parker always said that she traveled with enough clothing for a change of seasons, and that thought made her smile as she watched the two young men unload her four bags.

She unpacked her things and placed a picture of her and Jessica on the nightstand next to her bed. They were at the Waldorf Astoria for the Westchester County Women's Guild Winter Ball. They were on the dance floor together laughing. The photo had been taken more than four years ago, right before Parker died, and it was the last time she remembered being completely happy.

5

After an hour of sitting in her suite feeling sorry for herself, Olivia freshened her makeup and dressed for dinner. She took the elevator to the fourth deck and made her way to the banquet room. The room was elegantly adorned with white linen tablecloths, china, and fine crystal, its polished mahogany walls and glass chandeliers reminding her of The Millennium, her favorite restaurant in New York.

"Good evening, Mrs. Sagamore. How many are in your party tonight?" the maitre d' said.

"Good evening, party of one," she replied. For a moment she wondered how he knew her name, momentarily forgetting that she was wearing a nametag.

"Follow me, ma'am, I have a special place reserved just for you," the thin, balding man said as he guided her across the room to one of the round tables of eight.

"Good evening, Mrs. Sagamore. I'm Simon, and I will be serving you tonight. Would you like a cocktail?" the waiter asked, the second the maitre d' walked away.

"Hello Simon, nice to meet you. A cosmopolitan would be fine."

As quickly as he appeared, he was gone to fetch her drink. She took a sip of water while she waited, watching the other guests arrive. She noticed that there seemed to be some pattern to the seating arrangements, as she was still alone at her table until a tall, handsome man was shown to her table.

"Mr. Hamilton, this is Mrs. Sagamore. She will be your dinner companion this evening," the maitre d' said before slipping away.

Instantly recognizing him, she was startled. Rail-thin with a mahogany complexion and wavy black hair he stood a shade over six feet tall, his moustache neatly trimmed.

"Levi Hamilton, is it really you?" Olivia asked.

"Yes, it is," he replied in his rich baritone, assuming she was a random viewer who had recognized him. Some considered it a drawback, being on television five nights a week, with people recognizing you but you having no idea who they are. Levi Hamilton never minded the attention and felt that he owed it to the viewer to be accessible. The waiter brought her drink and Levi ordered a martini.

"Hi, there," he said turning on his anchor charm as he gently shook her hand.

"I'm going to jog your memory."

"Jog away."

"Peekskill Academy, class of 1966, you were the valedictorian."

"Yes, I graduated that year and I was the valedictorian," he answered, knowing she must have found the information in his bio on the East Coast Cable News website.

"So did I. Class of 1967," she said much to his surprise.

"From Peekskill?"

"Yes."

"Okay, let me think for a second," he said as the waiter quickly returned with his drink.

"Want a hint?"

"Okay, but just a little one."

"We used to work together a long time ago," she said with an impish grin.

"Really?"

"Yes."

"Let's see, it had to be before I went away to college," Levi pondered.

"No more hints coming from me."

"Olivia Cavillian - from the yearbook staff."

"Bingo!" Olivia squealed.

"I have to confess, I knew it was you all along," he said.

"No, way."

"Of course I did. You were quite the popular debutante. Captain of the women's swim team as I recall."

"Wow! You really do remember me."

"Yes, much more than you can imagine," Levi said. "How have you been?"

"Fine, how about you?"

"Not too bad."

"Are you here covering a big story? Should I pretend not to recognize you?"

"No, I'm just taking a short break before digging in for the fall ratings. So, what brings you here?"

"This trip is a gift from my daughter, son-in-law and my new grandchild-to-be."

"There is no way you are old enough to be a grandmother."

"You flatter me too much. Jessica is thirty-four and the baby is due in two months."

"Wow, doesn't time fly?"

"Yes, it does."

"Let's see, you married Parker Sagamore, right?"

"Yes, I did. He died four years ago."

"I'm sorry, I didn't know."

"It's alright. I've had time to deal with it. So what about you? Tell me about your wife and kids?"

"Not much to tell. I never married. I never had any children."

"Why not?"

"A combination of things. I went away to study journalism at the University of Missouri, then started work at a tiny station in Ft. Smith, Arkansas, after college. I followed that with stints in Baton Rouge, Tampa, Baltimore and Cleveland. I came back to New York from Cleveland when ECCN started up in 1987. I've been there for the past seventeen years anchoring the Ten PM Newshour."

"Sounds like you never had time to make a family?"

"I guess I never made the time."

"So, what's it like being a well-known newscaster?"

"I don't know about the well-known part, but it's a very challenging and satisfying job."

"What made you go into that field?"

"I like uncovering the truth. I have an insatiable curiosity, and it has served me well so far."

"Some people would call that just plain nosey," she said with smile."

"Oh, trust me, I am."

Noticing a lull in their conversation, Simon returned to take their order. They both settled on lobster tails. He ordered sugar snap peas and she decided on a baked potato with butter and extra sour cream. The waiter was back in minutes with fresh drinks and salads, and the two continued to renew their friendship.

"So what have you been doing with yourself over the years?" Levi asked as he munched on his salad.

"Parker and I ran an investment firm. Mainly international, but we handled some domestic ventures as well."

"So I'm sitting next to a financial wiz."

"Nope. I just sold the business. This old girl is officially retired."

"What do you plan to do now?"

"I plan on spoiling my grandchild rotten and being the world's greatest grandmother. Of course my daughter thinks that I should get married or as she puts it, 'get myself a man'."

"I'm starting to like that daughter of yours."

"Why, Levi Hamilton, are you flirting with me?"

"Yes, ma'am, I certainly am."

"Good. I like it."

The waiter returned with two fourteen-ounce lobster tails with melted butter. Steam rose from the plates as Simon sat the food before them. A man who had spent many years working at some of the east coast's finest restaurants, he deftly separated the tails from their shells and was gone, leaving the diners to enjoy their meal and each other's company. Eager to learn more about the intriguing woman next to him, Levi savored his meal and Olivia was equally curious about her dinner partner. They finished their main course and she settled on tiramisu for dessert. When the last dishes were taken away and Levi sipped a cup of coffee, she finally spoke.

"This is the first time I've been in a social setting with a man other than my husband."

"Really?"

"Yes."

"I take it that the two of you kept a full social schedule?"

"Oh, no. Parker never enjoyed social settings. He knew that public appearances were good for business, though, so he went along, always very careful to make sure I was well aware of his displeasure."

"How did you handle that?"

"He made it easy for me. Over the years as the company grew and he no longer felt the need to recruit new clients, he handed the responsibility of accompanying me to social functions to Jessica."

"So did she take after him or you?"

"I'm proud to say that she was and still is the spitting image of me. She eagerly took every chance to join the city's social elite. Truth be told, my time with her gave me much more pleasure than the time I spent with her father."

"I'm sorry to hear that."

"Oh, Levi, this must be boring you to tears. Let's talk about something else."

"I've got a better idea."

"Really?"

"Yes, c'mon, let's go."

He guided her by the hand out of the banquet room after stopping to chat with a Baltimore couple that recognized him from television. Olivia was amazed with the ease at which he handled the attention.

"Does it ever bother you when people you've never met before act as if they know you?" she asked when they were out of earshot.

"No, it's part of the territory. Every person you meet is a potential viewer, and they want to see if you're as friendly in person as you are on television," he said as they went out on the deck.

The two high school classmates were all smiles as they strolled under clear, starry skies. It was a warm night and the ocean breeze felt cool against Olivia's skin. In the distance they could see the lights of San Juan as *The Memphis* cruised just off the north coast of Puerto Rico. Holding hands as they walked along the upper deck, she felt more relaxed than she'd been in months. Just when Olivia thought the night couldn't have turned out better, things took another refreshing turn.

"Where are you taking me?" she asked.

"It depends," he answered.

"Depends on what?"

"It depends on whether or not you want to repay a debt?"

"A debt?"

"Yes, now it's time for *me* to jog *your* memory, madame."

"I'm listening."

"Years ago, we were in a yearbook staff meeting and as I recall, you promised me a dance."

"I did?"

"Yes, at the Snowflake Ball."

"Oh my," Olivia gushed. "In those days that ball was one of the biggest events of my life."

"Me too," Levi said. "I looked forward to it every December. It snowed eight inches my senior year."

"I remember," Olivia interrupted. "It was cancelled that year.

"Yes, it was. So, I didn't get my dance, and tonight I want it," he said as he opened the door to the nightclub.

As if she'd stepped out of reality into a fantasy world, Olivia took two steps inside and froze. This room was larger than the banquet room where they'd dined moments ago. There was a stage in front, a large dance floor in the middle, and several rows of horseshoe-shaped booths with round cocktail tables in the back of the room. On stage, immaculately dressed in red tuxedos, was one of her favorite musical acts - The Four Tops, belting out "I Can't Help Myself". The music was just as she remembered, complete with crisp dance moves and soulful voices.

"You seem a little surprised," Levi said, as she stood speechless.

"Did you know they would be here?" she asked after a long pause.

"Yes, I did. Wanna dance?"

Levi took her by the hand, spun her around and led her to the dance floor. Snapping her fingers and swinging her hips, she sang along and danced to the sweet sounds that had marked so many milestones in her life. "Baby, I Need Your Lovin'" was her favorite song, and she thought back to dancing in her room with her sisters and friends as the 45 played on her tiny phonograph. "If I Were A Carpenter" was the song she'd selected for the first dance with Parker on their wedding day, and "Ain't No Woman Like The One I Got" played on the radio the moment her daughter was conceived.

An hour flew by like seconds, as she delightfully glided through moves she hadn't used in years. Olivia and her partner never left the dance floor as the concert she hoped would never end wound down to the last song. She was wrapped tightly in Levi's arms, with her head on his shoulder. When she heard the stirring ballad, "I Believe in You and Me" Olivia realized on a cruise ship in the middle of the Caribbean, that she could fall in love again.

"Thank you, Jessica," she whispered as tears stung her eyes. It was the second time she had cried that day. This time they were tears of joy.

6

On the second day of her Caribbean cruise Olivia Sagamore woke up with an ear-to-ear grin. Feeling like a teenager, she sprang to her feet and turned on the shower. Levi had purchased her a copy of The Four Tops greatest hits CD that previous, glorious night. She popped the disk into the CD player on her nightstand and cranked up the sound, reliving the magical concert. The small bathroom filled with steam as she splashed water on her face and brushed her teeth.

She and Levi had enjoyed a wonderful evening together and had plans to meet for breakfast and then spend the day sightseeing and shopping in St. Croix. For years she had dreamed of vacationing in the Virgin Islands, and today she'd get her chance. She was getting dressed and singing along with the music when there was a knock at her door.

"Yes," she said as she turned the volume down, hoping it was Levi and that he was just as eager to see her, as she was to see him.

"I have a delivery for you, ma'am," a young man's voice said.

"Okay, just a second, please," she said, as she slid her arms inside her dress and opened the door."

What appeared to be a pair of legs topped by a massive bouquet stood before her.

"These are for you," he said, handing Olivia the vase.

"Oh, my!" She exclaimed, momentarily stunned by the bouquet of a dozen fresh-cut long-stemmed red roses. "Thank you."

"You're welcome."

"Wait one second," she said as she reached over and pulled a few bills from her purse.

"Thank you, ma'am."

"Thank *you*."

The young man walked away as she closed the door. Thinking the flowers were from her daughter, she opened the card. She smiled as read the simple note inside:

Olivia,
  Last night was wonderful. I can't wait to see you this morning.
Levi.

"What a wonderful thing to do," Olivia murmured.

She went to the bathroom to add some extra water, then set the vase on the table in the sitting room. Suddenly in an even brighter mood, Olivia shed the outfit she was wearing in favor of something a little brighter. The vibrant blue sun dress with yellow flowers was a gift from her daughter but Olivia had never worn it. She slipped the dress over her head and fluffed her hair. She looked in the mirror to check her makeup, much happier with what she saw.

The breakfast buffet was served outside on the observation deck above the swimming pools. Twelve tables of food were in place, with the standard breakfast fare of bacon, eggs, ham, potatoes, sausage and pancakes, ready for the taking. Patrons also had their choice of lox, bagels, made-to-order omelets and an ample selection of fresh fruit.

Olivia looked out over the ocean as the morning sunshine glistened off the beautiful blue water. The salty air filled her nostrils, and she marveled at the miles of wide-open water, a welcome change from the congestion of the city. Standing in the warm morning sun, she consciously waited for Levi. Within minutes he walked up and stood beside her.

"Hey, lady, can I buy you breakfast?" Levi said.

"Of course you can," she said as she threw her arms around his shoulders and hugged him. "By the way, thanks for the flowers. They are so beautiful."

"Flowers, I don't know anything about any flowers," he replied with a raised eyebrow.

"Well, I'll have to track down the man who sent them and give him a big kiss."

"Oh, well, since you put it like that, I plead guilty."

"Thanks, Levi. It's been a long time since anyone other than Jessica has sent me flowers," she said, hoping she didn't sound too pathetic.

"You're welcome. I just wanted to thank you for last night."

"It was more fun than I've had in years. I'm the one who should be thanking *you*."

"Wait until you see what I've got planned for you next."

"I don't think you can top last night."

"Oh, yeah, I've got a few more tricks up my sleeve."

"What are you up to Levi? I mean, we haven't laid eyes on each other in years."

"You're right, but I've thought of you often. I should have said something back in prep school but I never had the nerve."

"Are you trying to tell me that you had feelings for me that long ago?" Olivia asked.

"Yes."

"I had no idea."

"Well, now you do."

"So, what do you want from me now?"

"Right now I'm going to feed you, then I going spend the rest of the week romancing you."

"'Romancing,'" she said, then paused for a second. "That's a word I haven't heard in decades."

"Maybe it's time you did," he said, as he guided her to the buffet.

Olivia and Levi enjoyed breakfast as *The Memphis* cruised to its destination for the day, where people lined the dock and spilled into the streets. The large white ship provided a stark contrast to the lush tropical color of Christiansted Harbour. Adding to the hustle and bustle, merchandise vendors positioned themselves along the dock, ready to greet the tourists.

There was an air of excitement as the ship anchored and the passengers prepared to disembark. Olivia checked her watch. It was 10 a.m. and she was ready for adventure. She had planned a day of sightseeing with trips to Fort Christiansted, the Apothecary Museum, the Cruzan Rum Factory and the Cruzan Gardens on her agenda.

What Olivia didn't know was that Levi Hamilton had his own plans for her. Hand-in-hand they strolled down the ramp to blend into the throng waiting on the dock. It was a beautiful day and she was glad she had someone to share it with. Slowly making their way through the mass of people, they began their trek through the city.

They toured the fort and the museum where Alexander Hamilton once worked. Intrigued by the sweet smell of rum as they approached the rum distillery, Levi had a Caribbean Breeze and Olivia decided on an Islamorada Sunset once they were inside. More relaxed after their drinks, they took a guided tour of the Cruzan Gardens and were mesmerized by the large collection of rare and unusual tropical specimens.

"Dinner won't be served for another five hours. What sounds good for lunch?" Olivia asked.

"Anything would be fine with me. What about you?"

"I'm flexible."

"Good, because I've got an idea."

"You're up to something, aren't you?"

"Yes, I am, and I guarantee you'll like it."

"Okay, where are we going?"

"Back to the waterfront."

They took a taxi back to the harbor near the fort. There were many waterfront restaurants there and Olivia assumed they would choose one for lunch but, Levi was a step ahead of her. He led her past the restaurants and the two kept walking.

"We can wait here," he said once they reached the gazebo.

"If we're going to have lunch, shouldn't we go the other way?"

"Nope," he said with a wide grin.

Confused at his response, she shrugged her shoulders and took a seat. Staring out at the blue water, she fought hard to control the excitement building inside her. Five minutes later *The Enchantress*, a small yacht, floated their way.

"Ahoy, Mr. Hamilton!" the captain hailed from the bridge. "I trust you and your party are ready, sir!"

"How on earth did you arrange this?" Olivia asked in disbelief.

"Just a simple phone call. Come on, let's have lunch," he responded as he took her by the hand and led her toward the ship.

"Niles, it's good to see you again, old friend," Levi said once they were on board.

"Good to see you, Levi; it's been too long," Niles DeBeers said with a hint of Danish accent.

"Niles, let me introduce you to a good friend of mine, Olivia Sagamore."

"I'm pleased to meet you, madam. Any friend of Levi's is a friend of mine. Although I must say he has no other friends as lovely as you," Niles said.

"Thank you. It's nice to meet you."

"Now, you two, take a seat and we shall be off," Niles said as he engaged the engine.

"I'm dying to know how you arranged this?" Olivia whispered to Levi.

"You know what they say..."

"What?"

"Curiosity killed the cat."

The Enchantress set sail eastbound along the northern coast of St. Croix. Olivia admired the beautiful sea vistas as the boat moved along.

"Stella, old girl, we are on one heck of an adventure, aren't we?" Olivia thought to herself.

Suddenly a waitress bearing two glasses of wine appeared from the galley below. "Good afternoon, welcome to *The Enchantress*," she said as she extended the round serving tray. "On the menu today is conch chowder, a Caesar salad, and fresh mahi-mahi served island style with pungent local spices. For dessert we have key lime pie and Cruzan coffee"

"You have got to be kidding me," Olivia said turning to Levi.

"Not at all," he replied.

"We will arrive at Point Udall in ten minutes, and lunch will be served," the waitress said.

"What is Point Udall?" Olivia asked.

"It is the easternmost point of the United States. It's named for former Secretary of the Interior Stuart Udall. I came here a couple of years ago to cover the arrival of the new millennium. I did a live shot showing the sun first rising on American soil. I met Niles when I chartered his boat for the story," Levi answered.

"You are one smooth operator, you know that?"

"Yes, I do," he answered as he took a sip from his glass.

Within minutes they reached Point Udall and a lunchtime feast was served. As it turned out the waitress was Julie DeBeers. She and Niles joined Levi and Olivia for lunch. The four enjoyed a sumptuous Caribbean meal and two hours later *The Enchantress* returned to the harbor. Olivia and Levi did some souvenir shopping from the merchants along the dock before returning to *The Memphis*.

"May I join you for dinner tonight?" Levi asked before Olivia left for her cabin.

"You'd better, if you know what's good for you," she said before walking away.

Floating on a cloud of bliss, Olivia went back to her suite. She sat for a few minutes and decided to go to the communications center to send an email message to her daughter.

Jessica,

The trip is wonderful! I can't thank you enough. I hope you and the baby are fine. I'll be home Sunday and I'll call you. By the way, I ran into an old friend and we are having a great time. He's a guy I went to school with, prep school if you can believe that. Looks like Stella is definitely on the way to getting her groove back.

Love and kisses,
Mom

Olivia went back to her room to lie down for a while. It had been an eventful day and she needed a few minutes to recharge her batteries. She lay on the bed and looked at the photo of Jessica and herself on the nightstand. For her that was a very happy time, and now her joyous days had returned, thanks to Levi. These happy thoughts lulled her to sleep. After an hour-long nap she felt refreshed.

She arose and dressed for the evening wondering what surprises Levi had in store for her. Just as he had the night before, the maitre d' showed her to an empty table, Levi joined her minutes later, and the two of them dined alone together.

"My butt is going to be as wide as this boat if we keep eating like this," Olivia said as she finished her steak.

"Wide butt and all, you'll still be perfect to me," he said.

"Wow, you really know how to make a girl feel special."

"I do what I can."

"Before you even try, I've got to tell you that I'm too pooped for any of your big surprises tonight."

"No surprises here."

"Right."

"Scout's honor."

"So, you're telling me that you're done with me after dinner?" Olivia asked after Simon cleared away the dinner dishes.

"Well, I didn't say that."

"I knew it. What's up?"

"You'll have to follow me."

"Okay, I'm all yours."

As he had he night before, Levi led Olivia out into the moonlight. She stood in front of him wrapped tightly in his arms and listened to his heartbeat mixed with the sounds of the crashing waves. The sun was slowly setting and they watched the final rays give way to darkness punctuated by an array of stars. *The Memphis* cruised along through the Caribbean night as the couple climbed to the next level of the ship.

"So, am I in for another of your upper-deck surprises tonight?" Olivia queried.

"Yes, you are. Are you up for it?"

"Of course."

Stopping one level below where they'd gone the night before, they stepped inside The Circle Casino. Olivia looked around in wide-eyed wonder, startled momentarily by the lights and sounds of the machines. Hundreds of people filled the casino, all engaged in various games of chance. While it was difficult to tell who was winning or losing, it seemed they were all enjoying themselves.

"So what's your preference?" Levi asked, raising his voice above the clamor.

"I've never been to a casino before, I have no idea what to play," Olivia said.

"Okay, follow me. We'll try a little blackjack."

Following Levi over to a ten-dollar blackjack table, Olivia sat and watched a few hands before trying her own luck. An hour later she'd won eleven hundred dollars and Levi had lost six hundred bucks. They went from blackjack to roulette and then to poker. Poker proved to be too complicated for her, so they migrated over to the slot machines. The longer they played the different games, the more at ease she felt in the casino. Three hours after they entered the gaming center, the two left, four thousand dollars richer.

"Remind me to take you to Atlantic City once a month. With luck like yours I could quit my job," Levi said once they were outside.

"Maybe your luck is just beginning?" Olivia said with a raised eyebrow.

"What's that supposed to mean?"

"Now it's my turn to surprise you."

"So the lady has a mysterious side."

"Oh, yes, there's much more to me than meets the eye."

"So where are you taking me tonight?"

"It's a surprise, but I'll give you a hint."

"Okay."

"You are way overdressed," she said as she admired his black four-button suit and royal blue mock turtleneck sweater.

They strolled along the deck and went down to the pool level. There were a few people out for a late-night swim, but for the most part the area was empty. It was just what she wanted. She'd wanted to shock him as he much as he had surprised her.

"Take these, go in there and change, and I'll meet you here in five minutes," Olivia said as she nonchalantly reached into her purse and handed a pair of trunks to Levi.

"Wow!" he shouted, a little louder than he meant to. "When you plan a surprise you don't mess around."

"Mr. Hamilton, you have no idea what I'm capable of," she said as she pulled him close to her. "Now get in there and change."

Minutes later the two were sitting in a hot tub looking up at the stars over the Caribbean. The bottle of champagne Olivia had arranged for was waiting, and they sipped from the flutes and chatted while the warm water soothed their bodies.

"Okay Mr. Romance, I want the real scoop," she said cheerfully.

"What would you like to know?"

"I want to know the real reason why a man who moves the world around just to show a woman a good time isn't married already?"

"Well, my career..." he started.

"No way. It's got to be more than that," she interrupted. "Levi, you can be honest with me."

"Until I was in my late forties I never wanted to be married. I had plenty of opportunities, but I didn't want a wife and kids complaining because I was never there. Too many of my colleagues went through tough times because of the business. I knew I wanted to dedicate myself to my career, so that's what I did. Now I'm almost fifty-five years old and ready to get married, but most women my age are either happily married or happily divorced, and I refuse to be one of those pathetic old guys with a wife young enough to be his daughter. Plus, I'm way too old for changing diapers, late-night feedings, and play dates."

"So where's the girl who's waiting for you to settle down?"

"As much as I'd like to have her in my life, sadly for me, she doesn't exist."

"Now, tell me the real reason you are on this cruise alone?"

"I was ordered by my boss to take a week off to recharge my batteries for the rest of the campaign. With the election and the November sweeps coming up, I won't be able to take any more time off until after the holidays. I took a cruise so I would be isolated from news events, forced to relax and enjoy myself."

"Okay."

"You're pretty good with the questions."

"Hey, I'm a mom. I've had lots of practice."

"So now you won't mind answering a few questions for me," he said as he filled her flute.

"Ask away."

"What was the real issue between you and your husband?"

"Why do you ask?"

"Just a feeling that you left something unsaid."

"You're right," she said, her mood suddenly not so cheerful.

"I'm sorry, Olivia. If you'd rather not talk about it, it's okay."

"No, it's alright."

"Are you sure?"

"Yes, I'm sure," she said.

"Really it's none of my business," Levi backed off, knowing he had put a damper on the evening.

At ease and ready to unburden herself Olivia spoke, "You're right, Levi, there was a huge void between us. Many years ago, back in college, there was a guy in my life. This was before Parker and, just like you, he was respected and well known; and just like you, he was quite the charmer. He attended college out of state and we didn't see each other too often, but we were very much in love, or so I thought. Things happened very quickly, and on spring break during my senior year, I got pregnant. My family found out and they were furious. 'This is going to destroy the Cavillian name,' my father said."

"Did you know Parker then?"

"No, I met Parker right about the time I found out about the baby. He was ten years older and his first marriage had ended because he couldn't father children. His family was pressuring him about grandchildren and he was anxious to be married and raise a child. Jessica was born right before Christmas and we agreed not to tell anyone that Parker wasn't the biological father. He was very disappointed that she wasn't a boy so he wasn't a doting dad, but he raised her as his own. Parker was a very proud man from a proud family and on his deathbed he made me promise not to tell anyone the truth. He said Jessica was the only good thing to come from our marriage, except for the business, and he didn't want to lose her," she said sadly.

"Oh, my God. I had no idea," Levi said.

"It's okay, it feels good to get it out. This secret has haunted me for decades," she said. She took a deep, ragged breath and sipped more champagne.

"After all these years Jessica has no idea about her father?"

"I've tried on several different occasions to find the words but failed. Now, so much time has gone by. I know it's too late to tell her without losing her respect."

"Does the father know about Jessica?"

"No, I never told him."

"Are you still close to him?"

"Not really. I know where he is, but no, we're not close."

"I'm sorry I brought up such a painful time."

"Don't you want to know who he is?"

"No, it's not important."

"I want to tell you."

"Why?"

"Because I think we're on the brink of something special and I don't want there to be any silly secrets between us."

"I thought I was the only one feeling this. I'm relieved to know it's mutual. But knowing who her father is has no bearing on you and me."

"Are you sure?"

"Yes, I am," Levi replied as he took her in his arms. I know I care for you. That's enough for me."

7

High in the cloudfree eastern sky the bright yellow sun sat alone. Beautiful golden rays bounced off the deep blue ocean water and across the deck of the oceanliner. Before the requisite heat and humidity, that would certainly come, had time to build and make the day uncomfortable, the morning was breezy and mild. Olivia Sagamore sat pensive and anxious, waiting for her companion from the previous night to appear.

"Hey lady, did you finally dry out from last night?" Levi asked when he walked up to Olivia sitting in the radiant morning sun.

"I'm so glad you're here," she said, quickly to her feet, as she threw her arms around his broad shoulders.

He laid down his well-stocked backpack and asked, "Olivia, what's the matter?"

"I was afraid I wouldn't see you today after what I told you last night."

Levi gently cupped her face with both hands and looked deeply into her eyes. "Olivia, nothing you said last night changed how I feel. You told me more than you know."

"What do you mean?"

"To me, your complete honesty told me that you had complete faith in me to honor your secret. So, I can have faith in you, and I do."

"Are you sure?"

"Yes."

She took a reflective moment and softly asked, "Anything exciting planned for me today?"

"Yes, but you'll need to change your shoes," he said as he eyed the white sandals strapped around her ankles.

"Change my shoes?"

"Yes, put on something sturdy with heavy socks, and you need to eat something, you'll need your strength."

"Sounds good to me," she said with a slightly confused look.

The couple ate breakfast as *The Memphis* cruised near Castries along the northwest coast of St. Lucia. When the boat anchored they went ashore and took a taxi south to Soufriere to visit the world's only "drive-in" volcano, where pools of muddy water bubbled and steam clouds shot fifty feet into the air. They then hiked through the rainforest and made an upward climb of twenty-four hundred feet to the top of the Piton Mountains, where they enjoyed a light picnic.

"Are you ready for today's surprise?" Levi asked as he started to fill his backpack.

"You mean this isn't it?"

"Well, I guess we could call this part one."

"So what is part two?"

"First we go back to Castries, then I'll really show you something neat."

Five hours after they left, Olivia and Levi took a taxi back to where their day began and went to a small dive shop. Once inside Levi introduced her to a diving instructor, who looked to be a boy of fifteen or sixteen. As the two men began discussing diving equipment and diving spots, Olivia's curiosity got the better of her.

"Can you excuse us for a second?" Olivia said to the instructor.

"Levi, sweetie, what are we doing here?" she asked as she pulled him aside.

"Off the southern coast of Castries there is a wreck twenty feet below the surface. It is a great beginner's dive. We're going to get you some gear, give you a short diving lesson to certify you, and then you and I are going to take a dive."

"Really?" she said her eyes as big as saucers.

"Are you up for it?"

"I've never done anything like that before and I haven't gone swimming in years."

"But you were captain of the swim team."

"Yes, I was. Thirty-five years ago."

"You'll be fine. I'll be right beside you the whole time."

"Are you sure I can do this?"

"Of course you can."

An hour later, after being coached on the basic equipment and diving techniques, Olivia and Levi were taken by boat to their dive site. Side by side they slowly descended to the shipwreck site. Streaks of sunlight brightened the water near the surface, but as they dropped lower and lower into darkness headlights were needed. Twenty feet below sea level was a fifty-foot-long ship covered in black coral trees and large barrel sponges. With her head filled only with the sound of her breathing Olivia felt strangely at peace as she swam through the cool water.

A school of angelfish dappled by and prancing seahorses were among the dazzling cross-section of marine life they discovered below. Sunlight filtered through the crystal blue water illuminating the swaying leafy plants and brown jagged coral, as multi-colored fish swam by. A sea turtle lazily floated past the two divers barely acknowledging their prescence. Olivia was startled when Levi tapped her on the arm and showed her a three-foot-long, golden-spotted eel. The half-hour dive was over in what seemed like only seconds. They went up to the surface for a break and then down again for another half-hour before turning in their gear and returning to *The Memphis*, invigorated by the experience. One of Olivia's favorite things to do was watch a love story. That night Olivia and Levi shared a quiet dinner and went to the onboard movie theater. The cinema was showing *The Lancaster Affair*, a tale of two lovers in crisis. Cuddling in the dark theater, holding hands, and sharing a bag of popcorn was just as satisfying as anything Olivia had experienced since the trip began. After the movie Levi walked her to her suite and said goodnight.

"Don't you want to come in?" Olivia asked as she opened the door.

"Yes, I do. But I shouldn't," he said as he took a step back.

"You should, because it's what I want," she replied, pulling him closer.

"Olivia there is nothing in the world I want to do more right now than be with you. But I don't want you to look back with regrets. We don't have to rush into this, because I'm not going anywhere. I'll be around as long as you want me to be."

"I don't know what I did to deserve someone like you."

"Maybe it's your turn…maybe it's our turn."

"I hope you're right."

"Get some sleep. We have a busy day ahead tomorrow."

"Can I have a hint?"

"You'll need sturdy shoes, again."

"What am I going to do with you?" she asked as she playfully punched him in the arm.

"Keep me around," he said, before he kissed her goodnight and walked away.

After a long, arduous day they both slept soundly. On the fourth day of the cruise their plan was the same as the day before: breakfast together, and then a day of activity.

"What about my shoes? Will they do for today?" Olivia asked, wearing the same shoes from the day before.

"Not even close, but I'll take care of it," he answered.

"You always have all of your bases covered don't you?"

"Like the Boy Scouts say, be prepared."

"So are we cliff diving or bungee jumping today?'

"Neither, but you'll need your strength, so have a hearty breakfast."

After breakfast they left for a morning of sightseeing. Levi had arranged a 2 p.m. tee time at the Barbados Golf Club. The two were outfitted with shoes and clubs, then played eighteen holes on the PGA-quality course. After their round of golf they retired to a palm tree on the white sandy beach and enjoyed a couple of cool, fruity drinks before boarding the ship for dinner. Throwing caution to the wind, they both dined on steaks. Levi chose a New York strip and Olivia decided on a filet mignon.

After dinner Levi served up another surprise. They went to the nightclub next to the one where they'd danced to The Four Tops a few nights before. Onstage was a husband and wife were singing their rendition of Lionel Ritchie and Diana Ross' 'Endless Love' in the nightly, couples-only karaoke competition.

"How do you find these places?" Olivia asked.

"Oh, we journalists get used to digging," he said wryly.

"Don't tell me you're going to get up there and sing."

"I'm not. We are."

"What do you mean, 'we'?"

"I entered us in the competition. We have to find a song and get up and sing it."

"You are insane, you know that?"

"Lady, you have no idea how crazy I really am."

"How about 'I Got You Babe' by Sonny and Cher?" Olivia asked.

"Good choice."

A half-hour later the two Peekskill Academy graduates got on stage and belted out their chosen tune. Much to their surprise, their performance was good enough to make the finals. For the finals they chose 'You Don't Bring Me Flowers' by Neil Diamond and Barbra Streisand. It was one of Olivia's favorite songs, and their rendition was good enough for a second-place finish.

Day five of the southern Caribbean cruise dawned wet and stormy, causing the breakfast buffet to be moved into the banquet room. It was a scheduled day at sea for the ship and Levi and Olivia decided on a day of on-board shopping and relaxation.

"It looks like the tables have turned. Today you will be the one who needs the proper shoes," Olivia said as she sipped her coffee.

"What do you mean?" Levi asked.

"You never know much about a relationship until a man and woman go shopping together, so I'll be watching you carefully."

"I'll try to bear up under the pressure."

With a gift list as long as her arm, Olivia guided to the two-tiered shopping mall on the third level. She wanted to be sure to get some things for Jessica and the baby and she also wanted mementos of the trip for herself, as well as gifts for many of her former employees at Sagamore Investments International. While his list of needed items was not as lengthy as hers, Levi tended to be a slow shopper, agonizing over every decision. It would take the two of them a full day to make their purchases.

As the power-shopping excursion continued inside, heavy rain from nearby Tropical Storm Chris churned up the ocean and sent pounding waves crashing against the hull of *The Memphis*. A sturdy sea vessel built to endure much stronger storms, the forty-five mile-per-hour winds were of no consequence and went practically unnoticed by the passengers on board as the ship moved on toward St. Johns, Antigua.

Three hours after they began, Olivia and Levi dropped off the first load of packages in their respective suites. Settling on a couple of salads, they enjoyed a light lunch before heading back to the mall. The shopping continued until nearly 4 p.m. when Olivia was paged on the mall public address system.

"Hi, there; I'm Olivia Sagamore - someone paged me?" she said to the man in the information booth.

"Yes ma'am, one second," he said as he checked his computer screen.

"What's going on?" Levi asked when he walked up.

"Mrs. Sagamore, you have an urgent message waiting for you in the communications center," the man said.

"Thank you," she said and hurried in the direction he indicated.

Levi caught up with her as she reached the room. "I know it's tough, but try to stay calm," he said as he took her hand reassuringly.

"I'm afraid it's the baby. Jessica isn't due for another two months."

Olivia and Levi hurried to the communications center, where she received the message that would shake her to the core.

"I'm Olivia Sagamore. You have an urgent message for me," she said to the young woman who had helped her send an e-mail to Jessica a few days earlier.

"Mrs. Sagamore," said a voice behind her. "I'm ship captain John Gruenwald. We met at dinner a few days ago and this is Dr. Wilson Keppler, the medical chief of staff. We have your message. Please come with us."

Olivia was taken into the doctor's office, a tiny space, with room for only a desk and a couch. Captain Gruenwald sat on the edge of the front of the desk, Dr. Keppler sat in his chair. Olivia took a seat on the couch next to Levi and clutched his hand as she was given the news.

The captain spoke first, "Mrs. Sagamore, earlier today there was an automobile accident in New York involving your daughter."

"Oh, my God! Olivia screamed. "Is she alright?"

"No, ma'am, I'm afraid she's not. She suffered a crush injury when her car was broadsided by a loaded eighteen-wheeler. Afterward, she was trapped in the car for two hours, and had to be cut out by the Jaws of Life."

The room was silent as the captain's words raced across Olivia's mind. *"This can't be true," she thought.*

"No, please God." Olivia prayed. "Not my baby."

Dr. Keppler then added, "Since she is pregnant her general filtration rate is higher due to increased blood volume, and the obstruction caused her kidneys to fail. She has been placed on dialysis until her kidneys begin to function again."

"I've got to get home. My baby needs me."

The captain spoke again, "Right now Tropical Storm Chris is bearing down on the Caribbean, but current forecasts from the ship's meteorologist indicate that you will be able to fly out tomorrow. The ship will dock in Antigua and first thing tomorrow morning a chartered plane will fly you back to New York."

"Why can't I leave now?

"The winds from the tropical storm are too strong, or we'd charter a helicopter to take you to the nearest island. I'm afraid tomorrow morning is the best we can do."

Olivia broke down and buried her face in Levi's chest. He held her tightly and fought back tears of his own. "What if Jessica's kidneys fail to begin functioning normally?" Levi asked.

"Then she will need an immediate transplant," the doctor replied.

"I feel so helpless doctor. Is there anything I can do?" Olivia asked.

"Kidney cross-matching is done by matching HLA, human leukocyte antigens, through the blood and I'd like to draw a sample from you. I can fax the results to the hospital in New York and we'll know whether you and your daughter are a match, just in case she eventually needs a transplant."

"Is that likely?"

"No. In the majority of cases like these the kidneys resume normal function after a short time. The HLA match is just a precautionary measure."

"I'm ready."

Dr. Keppler drew a blood sample and prescribed a mild sedative for Olivia. Devastated by the news from home, Olivia went back to the communications center and called her son-in-law, Brad. She reached him on his cell phone at the hospital. He was in the waiting room outside Jessica's room in ICU.

"Brad, it's Mom. How is she?"

"Not good, Mom. Her car was crushed and she was in there for a long time. The doctors say that if her kidneys don't start functioning soon, they'll have to do a transplant or take the baby by C-section."

"Has she been placed on the organ donor list?"

"Yes."

"Well, that's just a precaution, we won't worry about that. Jessica is a very strong woman."

"They say she could die, Mom. I'm scared I'm going to lose both of them," he said as he broke down for the first time since learning of the accident.

"That's not going to happen, Brad. We both know how stubborn she can be."

"Yeah, she's pretty stubborn, he said as a chuckle replaced his tears.

"You be strong and try not to worry. I'll be home tomorrow."

"I'm sorry about ruining your vacation."

"Nonsense, I'll be there soon. In the meantime, you give her a kiss for me."

"Okay."

After Olivia spoke with Brad, Levi escorted her to her suite. When the day began, she had been full of hope and her biggest worry was whether she would be able fit all the gifts she'd purchased into her luggage. Now she had a much more onerous bundle of worries. She opened the door to her suite, walked in and slumped into a loveseat in the sitting room.

"Olivia, I don't think you should be alone tonight," Levi said as he sat down next to her.

"I'm alright. I wouldn't be good company tonight."

"Please don't make me leave?" he begged.

"Frankly Levi, I'd rather be alone."

"Okay, but on one condition," he said as he knelt before her. "You'll let me go back to New York with you tomorrow."

"Would you really?" Olivia asked, sounding relieved. "I hate interrupting your vacation, but I could really use some support right now."

"I want to be by your side."

"Oh, Levi," she sighed with relief as she wrapped her arms around him.

"I'll meet you tomorrow morning at seven."

"I'll be packed and ready to go."

"Good. I'll leave you alone now, but if you need me don't hesitate to call," he said before rising and walking to the door.

"I promise, I'll be fine."

"Goodnight, Olivia."

"Goodnight."

After Levi left for his suite Olivia sat for a while and shed a few tears for her daughter. After ten minutes of the sound of nothing but her own weeping she turned on the television. Not in the mood for news, she tuned to the Lifetime Movie Network, where one of Charlie's Angels was dealing with a cheating husband. Olivia needed the distraction as she emptied the closet and drawers and began packing.

Not realizing how much clothing she'd brought along until now, she stuffed her luggage and completed her task in a half-hour. It was only a few minutes past 7 p.m., but she decided to skip dinner and turn in early. She changed into her nightclothes, took off her makeup, and was brushing her teeth when there was a knock at the door.

"Yes," she answered, thinking that Levi had returned.

"Room service," came the voice from the other side of the door.

"I didn't order room service."

"Mr. Hamilton ordered it for you, ma'am."

Olivia opened the door and the table was wheeled in. Under covered containers on fine china was a small garden salad with French dressing, baked chicken with creamed spinach and whole kernel corn, and cheesecake for dessert. The table was adorned with a white cloth and a bouquet of fresh flowers as the centerpiece. Olivia gave the steward a tip and sat down for a quiet dinner. She didn't have much of an appetite, but she appreciated Levi's consideration. After a few bites of food she pushed the table outside her cabin, turned off the television, and went to bed.

After a few fitful hours where sleep was elusive, she gave up and threw on her robe. She went down the corridor and took the elevator up one level. On the third deck she walked along the corridor, ignoring odd looks from the other passengers dressed for dinner, dancing, and other nightly activities. Arriving at her destination, she knocked at the door, and could hear the sounds of a baseball game coming from the television. When Levi opened the door, her mood brightened immediately.

"Want some company?" Olivia asked apprehensively. "I can't sleep."

"Of course, Olivia, come in."

"I know you wanted to stay and I said I wanted to be alone, but I feel like I have no one else in the world right now but you," she said as she collapsed in his waiting arms.

"You're not alone, and we are going to get through this together. I'm going to be beside you all the way," he said as he stroked her hair.

"I'm sorry you got dragged into all this."

"Olivia, you're not dragging me into anything."

"Really?"

"Yes, really."

They sat down and switched the channel to a movie. Levi ordered two bottles of wine and they nestled on the couch until she fell asleep an hour later. He waited until she was in a deep sleep before carrying her into the bedroom. He tucked her in with great care before going to lie down on the couch. Drained from what had been a very active week, Levi was asleep in minutes.

Olivia's slumber was far from peaceful. The nightmare began with her standing on the deck of *The Memphis* and Jessica floating in the ocean. Olivia couldn't swim and seemed to be alone on the ship. Reaching out her hand in the darkness, she screamed as she helplessly watched her child floating farther and farther away. Startled by the dream she abruptly woke up at 3 a.m. with an unshakable feeling that Jessica needed her. She was sitting in bed with her tear-stained face in her hands when Levi, awakened by her sobbing, rushed into the room.

"Olivia, I know this must be horrible for you, but try not to worry," he said as sat on the edge of the bed. "We'll be there soon."

"I hate not being there when I know she needs me."

"She's going to be fine, you'll see."

"I hope you're right."

"I am," he said, before rising to his feet. "Now you try to get back to sleep."

"Where are you going?"

"Back to the couch."

"No, stay here with me," she said reaching out and taking his hand.

"Are you sure?"

"Yes, just stay here and hold me," she said as she pulled him into the bed.

They curled up in the queen-sized bed and slept for another three hours before waking and getting dressed for the trip that would change their lives forever. Light rain was still falling and when they arrived on deck, Captain Gruenwald and Dr. Keppler were there to meet them.

"Good morning, Mrs. Sagamore," the captain began. "I'm terribly sorry about your daughter. A car is ready to transport you and Mr. Hamilton to V.C. Bird International Airport, where a plane is waiting for you. You will land at LaGuardia four hours after takeoff."

"Thank you for arranging this for me."

"No problem, ma'am."

"What about the tropical storm?" Levi asked as he eyed the raindrops.

"Early season storms are often weak, and this one has already been downgraded to a depression," the captain said.

"At least we won't have to deal with that," Levi said.

"Oh, shoot, I forgot my watch," Olivia said as she checked her wrist.

"I'll go and get it for you," Levi said.

"No, I'll go," she answered. "I'd lose my head if it wasn't screwed on."

"Take the umbrella. I'll wait here for you."

"I'll only be a minute," she said before darting off.

With her mind two thousand miles away, Olivia mumbled to herself as she quickly walked with the umbrella in her right hand. She grabbed the railing with her left hand and started down the steps. She had taken only two of the twenty-four steel steps when her left ankle twisted and her right foot slipped. Levi and the other two men jerked around instantly as Olivia let out a loud scream.

"Olivia!" Levi screamed as she began to tumble out of control, dropping lower from sight.

Olivia made a futile attempt to grab the railing but her awkward fall continued. She flipped head-first over the railing and landed hard on the deck twenty feet below. A small pool of blood spread from where her head met the surface of the ship. The three men scrambled down the stairs where they found her limp and unconscious.

"Wilson, what should we do?" Captain Gruenwald asked, grimly.

"Don't move her yet. Get two of the nurses to assist me," the doctor answered.

"I'll get right on it," the captain said bounding up the steps two at a time.

"Dr. Keppler, how bad is it?" Levi asked as he helplessly stared at her lying motionless before him.

"I'm not sure, Mr. Hamilton. She took quite a fall," the doctor said as he checked her pulse and breathing.

"How can I help?"

"Just try to be patient until I can diagnose her condition."

"Should we move her to the hospital in Antigua?"

"Mr. Hamilton we have better medical facilities on-board than in Antigua, but we are not a level-one trauma center."

"Is that what she needs?"

"Yes, I'm afraid so."

"So let's put her on the plane to New York," Levi said, his voice showing none of the calm normally present on the evening news.

"We have to stabilize her condition first," Dr. Keppler said as the nurses arrived.

Olivia was lifted on a gurney and taken to the medical center where Dr. Keppler bandaged her wound. He treated her for over two hours and took special care to stabilize her blood pressure, breathing, and temperature. Her EEG results showed diminished brainwaves and as near as the doctor could tell she had suffered a subdural hematoma, and was in a coma.

"Mr. Hamilton, come with me please," Dr. Keppler said to Levi in the waiting room three hours after Olivia had fallen.

"Sure," Levi said as he rose to his feet with none of the boundless energy he had shown recently.

The two men walked into the doctor's office and Dr. Wilson Keppler gave the darkest diagnosis he'd given in his twelve years as a cruise ship medical director. In a typical day his medical regimen consisted of bandaging cuts and scrapes or, on a more serious day treating sea sickness or the flu. But this was well beyond anything he'd encountered before.

"Mr. Hamilton, I've stabilized Mrs. Sagamore, but she has suffered a closed brain injury. She has a blood clot on the left side of her brain. If it hemorrhages, she could die. Right now she's in a coma, but we need to relieve the pressure. Our facilities are superior to what's in Antigua, but we aren't equipped for the level of care she needs and I don't have the expertise to perform the procedure.

Moving her right now is risky, but her only hope lies in Miami. I've taken the liberty of arranging medical transport to Jackson Memorial Hospital, the only level-one trauma center in south Florida. The helicopter will be here in two hours and will fly the three of us in."

"Is there anything I can do?" Levi asked.

"Pray."

8

The only way Jeff Burris would become more powerful than Roderick Schilling was to win the presidency. Still smarting from the verbal cuffing he'd received at the governor's conference in Indianapolis, he attacked the campaign trail at a torrid pace. Tirelessly crisscrossing the nation, he worked with intensity never before seen.

In spite of his monumental efforts, he still trailed President Greenlee by eleven percent in the polls. After a fund-raising luncheon in Cleveland, where he hoped his coattails would help elect Clayton O'Neal as Ohio's first African American governor, he was off to a dinner in Columbus, Ohio, and a private meeting with Senator Eddie Blanton. It was meeting he dreaded but had to attend.

"My fellow Americans, I say to you tonight, if you want four more years of the status quo - four more years of a stagnant economy, high unemployment, and weak foreign policy - then by all means cast your vote for the incumbent. But if you share a vision of a nation with its economic and social vitality re-energized, then go to the polls and cast your vote for the Constitution Party. Senator Blanton and I appreciate your support," Jeff Burris said to a rousing round of applause.

The two men stood and shook hands with each other, then joined hands with Clayton O'Neal, and the three of them posed with their clasped hands held high. With another Kodak moment behind him, Jeff Burris moved on to the meeting. A half-hour later he and Eddie Blanton met face to face.

"Eddie, I'll be honest with you. You weren't my choice for vice president but Roderick Schilling forced the issue. Nothing personal against you, but I didn't think you were a good fit with me. Now that you're on the ticket, I expect nothing but your best effort and full cooperation with me and my staff."

"Jeff, I gave my word at the convention that I would do whatever was necessary, and I've been doing that. I know that you wanted Ward Cargellon as your running mate. I'm sorry he turned it down."

"What do you mean, turned it down?"

"I was at a meeting in June with Cargellon and Schilling. Roderick offered him the spot but Ward said no. He didn't want to run because he didn't think you could beat Greenlee."

"If that's the case, why did you accept the nod?"

"I could have gone to Notre Dame and played in the shadow of Touchdown Jesus, but I chose Ohio State because the program needed a shot in the arm. I won a national championship there. When Cleveland drafted me, the worst team in the league, I took them to two championships. The reason I'm on the ticket is simple: I like the underdog, and I like a good fight."

"What makes you think I'm the underdog?"

"Please don't take this the wrong way, Jeff, but you have absolutely no appeal to voters east of the Mississippi. I've seen the research on your candidacy, and it doesn't look good. The only reason I'm not the presidential nominee is that the party felt I needed more time on the national stage. Schilling thinks that if I run for vice president now and we lose because you are a weak candidate, that in four years I'll be the presidential nominee and you'll be off writing your memoirs and speaking on the banquet circuit."

"You pompous jerk! Who do you think you're talking to?"

"You got lucky with one case in California and you milked it all the way to the governor's office. Unless I pull out a miracle, your political career is over. Face it, Jeff; your own party doesn't believe in you. I'm the only hope you've got."

"You'll do what you're told."

"Don't flatter yourself. I didn't get this far in life being intimidated by the likes of you and I'm not about to start now."

"This is politics, not football."

"Jeff, once you've stood in a packed stadium in front of a hundred thousand people who want you to fail and faced down jacked-up, two hundred seventy-five pound linebackers who want to rip your head off, loudmouth lawyers in cheap suits don't faze you, and that's all you are to me. So here's what we're going to do if you want me on the ticket. Your staff can send itineraries to mine. Joint appearances are fine but, hey, that's up to you. I've got my own plane so we can travel separately," he said confidently.

"I think you are forgetting who's the presidential nominee and who's the vice-presidential nominee."

"Jeff, no one thinks you can beat Greenlee. The party is counting on me. All I have to do is make one phone call to Schilling and you're off the ticket. If you don't believe me, call him yourself - but don't say I didn't warn you."

"Maybe I'll make that call," Jeff Burris said as he reached for the phone.

"Suit yourself," the well-muscled senator said as he strolled briskly out of the room.

9

Olivia Sagamore had first come to Miami five days earlier, flying first-class on a DC-10. This time she arrived via a Lifeline helicopter with a team of doctors working frantically to keep her alive. Her condition had not changed since her fall. She was still comatose, and emergency surgery was scheduled as soon as the chopper landed.

"Let's get her inside as fast as we can," Dr. Wilson Keppler said as the helicopter touched down.

"How is she?" the paramedic asked.

"She's stable tight now, but I have no idea for how much longer. I've got her X-rays and test results."

"Let's move!"

Within minutes Olivia Sagamore was wheeled into the trauma center, where her X-rays and test results were quickly analyzed. Dr. Keppler's diagnosis was correct and Olivia was immediately taken into surgery, where a team was scrubbed and ready. All the while, Levi sat in agony in the waiting room. He waited until Dr. Keppler gave him an update before making a call to Brad, Olivia's son-in-law. He knew the young man was already under extreme duress and hated to add to it, but under the circumstances he felt he had no choice.

"Hi, Brad, this is Levi Hamilton, an old friend of Olivia's. I was on the cruise with her," he began.

"Yes sir, do you know if she caught her flight back to New York?"

"No, she didn't," Levi said. He paused and bit his lip before saying the words he hated to utter. "There's been an accident."

70

"Accident?" Brad said as if he'd never spoken the word before. "Is she alright?"

"I'm sorry to say that she isn't. We just landed in Miami. Olivia is in surgery."

"Surgery! What happened?"

"She fell, aboard ship and landed hard on her head. She's in a coma. The doctors are trying to release the pressure on her brain."

"Oh my God," Brad sighed. "What am I going to tell Jess?"

"How is Jessica?"

"She's still in ICU"

"For now, let's not tell her about her mom. Just tell her Olivia is on the way."

"I can't lie to her."

"Do you really think telling her the truth is best right now?"

"Probably not."

"Brad, I'm sorry to lay all of this on your shoulders, but I thought you should know. I'll be here with Olivia and I'll call you as soon as she is out of surgery."

"Thanks."

Levi hung up the phone and went in search of a strong cup of coffee. He walked down the hall and took note of the pain in the faces he passed. He had been to various medical centers all across the world covering news stories. In his role as a newsman he had always been able to remain detached, and since he had no family Levi had not been in hospital for a personal matter since he broke his arm in seventh-grade gym class. Now, years later, he was back; but this time the stakes were much higher.

After all the years of waiting for the right woman to come along he refused to give in to his fear of losing her. The minutes turned to hours as he drained cup after cup of the steamy brew. He tried to eat but had no appetite. It was 4 p.m., Olivia had been in surgery for over three hours and still there was no word on her condition. He called Brad again with nothing new to report but promised to call when he knew more.

An hour later Levi sat in the waiting room and watched the evening news. The presidential campaign was the top story, with President Greenlee maintaining a five-percent lead in the polls over Jeff Burris. Normally one who thrived on political news, the story didn't interest him in the least.

Levi sat through the accounting of the day's crimes, accidents and weather reports, giving only minimal attention to the fancy graphics and bold music that flashed by. Oddly enough, the story of one of New York's prominent businesswomen being airlifted to Miami's Jackson Memorial Hospital was left out.

"God, I hate local news," he muttered as he crumpled his empty coffee cup in disgust.

"Mr. Hamilton," a slumping man said as he stretched his arm and extended his aching hand. "I'm Doctor Givens. I just performed surgery Mrs. Sagamore."

"Is she all right?" Levi said as he jumped to his feet.

"Come with me, sir, and I'll fill you in."

The two men walked down the hall to the doctor's office where Givens described the six-hour surgical procedure and gave Levi the bleak prognosis for Olivia's recovery. Levi sat and listened and, having a much larger understanding of medicine than the doctor anticipated, had a few questions of his own.

"When Olivia was examined on the ship by Dr. Keppler, he gave her a Glasgow Coma Score of five. I know that three is the worst and fifteen is the best."

The nature of the query spiked the doctor's curiosity. "So do you have a working knowledge of medicine?" he asked.

"Yes, before I became an anchor I was a medical reporter in Cleveland," Levi answered. "How is she doing now?"

"Through the surgery we managed to relieve the cranial pressure and repair her ruptured blood vessels, which stopped the bleeding. Unfortunately her best eye response remains at two, and her best verbal response remains at one, although her best motor response rose to three."

"So she's only at six," Levi sighed.

"That gives her a sixty-three percent chance of survival."

"I thought she'd get better with the surgery. When can we expect improvement?"

"The next twenty-four hours will be the most critical."

"I don't know if you're aware of the fact that her daughter is in renal failure in New York. Jessica is seven months pregnant and unless she undergoes a transplant soon, neither she nor the baby will make it."

"Yes, I'm aware of that. As a matter of fact I spoke to the doctors at Manhattan General before Mrs. Sagamore arrived. Dr. Keppler advised me that he had already tested her human leukocyte antigens on the ship. We compared our results to his and she is a compatible HLA match for her daughter."

"How many points?"

"Six out of six."

"But you can't do the transplant until she comes out of the coma?"

"Yes, that's correct."

"So what's next?"

"I'm sorry, but we've done all we can do. The rest is up to her."

10

"Roderick, Jeff Burris here. I've got a problem with Blanton," he said curtly.

"What's the problem?" the Constitution Party Chairman said as he muted the Minnesota Twins game on the television.

"I want him off the ticket."

"Not that again."

"I'm the nominee, it's my call."

"No, Jeff, I'm the party chairman. *It's my call.*"

"You may be the party chairman but I'm making this decision."

"Let's get a few things straight, Jeff. You're not making any decisions about anything. You'll be lucky if you make a respectable showing against Greenlee."

"I won the governor's office of the largest state in the union by a landslide," Jeff said in a confrontational tone.

"You won because I leaked pictures of your opponent in a compromising position with his seventeen-year-old babysitter," Roderick said matching Burris' tone, his anger building by the second.

"I'm still the nominee."

"You're the nominee because I made you the nominee. I handpicked you, and matched you with Blanton for the Constitution Party's benefit, not yours. Ward Cargellon was my first choice, but he wants to be part of a winning ticket and he knew you couldn't pull it off. So you will run and you will lose. In four years we'll pair Blanton and Cargellon, and we will win. Blanton is the future of the party - and if you do anything to screw this up, I'll ruin you."

"You've got nothing."

"Sure I do Jeff. We did some checking into your collegiate years and we found dirt...paydirt, actually"

"You're bluffing."

"Try me," Roderick said before abruptly hanging up.

11

Brad quietly walked into the room and sat by his wife's side. He had just finished a phone conversation with Levi and was fully advised of Olivia's post-operative state. Although Jessica's kidneys were still not functioning her condition had improved and Brad knew the time had come to tell her about her mother. But watching her sleep so peacefully, he decided to wait until the next morning.

At six-thirty the next morning Jessica awoke and looked over at Brad and smiled. It was her third day in the hospital, and the first night she'd had an episode around 3 a.m. This time she'd slept the whole night through. He was asleep and she imagined that their soon-to-be-born daughter would look the same way. She reached out and pulled his jacket up a little higher to keep him warm. Feeling her touch, he opened his eyes and saw that a little of her color was coming back.

"Hi, how are you feeling?" he asked.

"I'm fine, and so is the baby, she said gently rubbing her tummy.

"You've got to get some sleep. Why don't you go home for a little while?"

"I'm fine. If I went home I'd just worry, so I'm better off here with you two."

"How sweet of you to worry about me, but I'm fine."

"Babe I have something to tell you." He said as he took her hand.

"Is the baby alright?" Jessica asked, her eyes filling with panic.

"No, it's not the baby. It's your mother."

"Mom's still on the cruise."

"No, she's not. There's been an accident."

"What kind of accident?"

"She slipped down some stairs on the ship and fell."

"Is she alright?"

"No." After a long pause he spoke. "She's in a coma."

Brad relayed the information Levi had given him over the phone about Olivia's condition before and after the surgery. Dr. Richard Orland, chief of staff of Manhattan General, entered the room just as Brad gave Jessica the horrible news. She was shaken by what she had heard and understandably upset.

"Do you have any questions about your mother?" Dr. Orland asked.

"Yes. How soon can she be transported back to New York?"

"I wouldn't recommend moving her for a few days. It is best to make sure her condition is stabilized first."

"I'd worry a lot less if she were here with me."

"Oh, we wouldn't be able to place the two of you in the same room. All rooms in ICU are private rooms. Besides, hospital policy requires separate care for comatose patients."

"I don't care what your rules are, I want my mother here, in this room, with me. Which part of that do you not understand?" Jessica said forcefully.

"Calm down, Jess, he's got a job to do," Brad said.

"I don't care about his job. I want my mother here as soon as possible, and I won't take no for an answer. Either you do it at this hospital or I'll go somewhere else."

"I'll see what I can do," the doctor said. "But there is another pressing matter we need to discuss."

"Please, go on," Brad said.

"Your baby is two months premature and weighs approximately four pounds. With you in renal failure it would be a huge risk, but we could take her now. The lungs develop last, and at thirty-two weeks hers aren't fully developed, so she wouldn't be able to go home for a while. It would be a struggle for her, but we have the top neo-natal unit on the East Coast," the doctor said.

"There is no way you're taking my baby," Jessica said defiantly.

"What's our other option?' Brad asked.

"Jessica stays in the hospital until her kidneys regain function. She will have to deliver by C-section and then we can perform a transplant if it becomes necessary. Your mother is a perfect match, but we have to wait until her condition improves," answered Dr. Orland.

"Jessica, what do you want to do?"

"I'm keeping my baby right where she is, thank you," Jessica said pursing her lips and placing a protective hand on her tummy.

"I think you should reconsider," Dr. Orland said.

"There is nothing to think about. This little girl is going to have a fighting chance, and I'm going to make sure of it," she said firmly. "Now, why don't you get started on finding a room suitable for me and my mother."

"Honey, calm down."

"I don't think so, Bradley, and give me your cell phone," she said, using the name that told him she was upset. "I'll call mom's lawyer and we'll see about getting her moved here."

The two defeated men left the room as she angrily punched the numbers on the phone.

"Wow, she is a spitfire," the doctor said once the two men reached the hallway.

"No, doctor, I beg to differ. She's a raging inferno!"

Two days later at a cost of twenty thousand dollars via a specially outfitted medical transport plane, Olivia Sagamore and Levi Hamilton were flown from Miami to New York. Harry Fields chartered the air ambulance, was at LaGuardia when the plane landed and escorted his client to her room at Manhattan General.

Her condition was stable and her Glasgow Coma Score was still at six. Levi had been by her side the whole time and was there when Olivia was wheeled into her room. He had seen pictures of Jessica and spoken to Brad over the phone; now they met face to face.

"Hello, I'm Levi Hamilton. I went to prep school with Olivia," he said as he shook hands with Brad.

"Thanks for calling me, sir. Jessica and I really appreciate it," Brad said.

"I only wish it were under happier circumstances."

"Mr. Hamilton, thank you for staying with mom," Jessica said from her bed.

"Jessica, I've heard so much about you," Levi said as he walked across the crowded room as two medical technicians connected monitors to Olivia's bed. "Wow! You look just like your mother during her Peekskill Academy days."

She reached out and hugged him and motioned for him to sit down on the side of the bed.

"Please tell me what happened to mom?" Jessica asked tearfully.

"She was in a hurry and she fell down a flight of stairs and hit her head on the deck of the ship."

"Did she know about my car accident?"

"Yes, we found out the day it happened but we couldn't fly out immediately because of a tropical storm. We were set to leave the next morning and she had forgotten her watch."

"She always did that."

"'I'll only be a minute,' were the last words your mother spoke to me," Levi said as tears welled in his eyes.

"I got an e-mail from her, apparently you two were having quite a time," Jessica said trying to brighten his mood.

"Yes, we were. We went dancing, gambling, shopping, golfing, hiking...even scuba diving."

"Wait a minute; you took my mother scuba diving?" she said in surprise.

"Yes, and she loved it so much we went down for a second dive."

"I can't believe you got her to do that."

"I even persuaded her to enter a karaoke contest."

"On stage, singing? That does not sound like my mother at all."

"She was a good sport. We both had a great time."

"Thank you for taking care of her for me."

"Jessica, your mother is very special to me. Not only do I plan to be at her side when she wakes up but beside her each day for the rest of our lives."

"I'm glad you're so sure she's going to make it, Mr. Hamilton. That makes two of us."

12

Sitting on the desk in Levi Hamilton's tiny office at the East Coast Cable Network was a plaque. The inscription read: *When the going gets tough, the tough get going. - Joseph Kennedy.*

For Levi Hamilton, when the going got tough, he went to work. It was the one place where he felt totally in control, and control was something he desperately needed. A million thoughts ran across his mind as the taxi meandered through the midday traffic toward the ECCN studios.

The prognosis from Dr. Orland was bleak. He gave Olivia only a forty percent chance of full recovery, and the odds of her regaining enough strength to survive a kidney transplant surgery were slim. Levi knew in his heart that Olivia would recover, but he wasn't so sure she'd heal soon enough to help her daughter.

"You're not supposed to be here, Levi. You're supposed to be on vacation," Bureau Chief Ned Madigan's voice bellowed across the room.

"Then pretend you don't see me," Levi said before slamming the door to his office and turning on his computer. He put on a pot of coffee and called the research department.

"Hi Sharla, it's Levi Hamilton. I need some help," he began.

"I thought you were on vacation," she replied.

"You know how it is, you get a few days off, then they call you back in."

"Yuck! Don't you just hate that?"

"Oh, yeah, but what can I do. Anyway, I need travel itineraries for the Constitution Party nominees. I need to track them down for a couple of interviews for a story I'm working on."

"They should be fairly easy to find. They release their every move so we can be there for photo opportunities."

"They'll do anything for free publicity."

"Yes, they will. Give me a few minutes to look up the info and I'll call you right back."

"Thanks," Levi said before hanging up.

He logged on to the Internet and began a search. Working with the skill of a private investigator, he moved from one website to another, searching for knowledge. Ten minutes later the phone rang and, armed with the information he needed, Levi Hamilton left his office. He stopped by the hospital to visit Olivia and Jessica before heading to LaGuardia for a flight to Detroit, where the nominee was speaking at a fund-raising dinner.

Four hours after Levi left his office the plane touched down. Although the calendar said late August, the wind whipping around him as he waited for a taxi spoke more of fall than summer. Levi was reminded of his years in Cleveland where autumn came in August and winter arrived in October. Once he reached the convention center, a few quick flashes of his press ID allowed him to get inside. He waited until the speech was finished and positioned himself among the other reporters covering the campaign stop.

After the speech was made, his security team led Jeff Burris to the pressroom for a few questions. Tim Reynolds, the Burris/Blanton campaign manager, spotted Levi and came over to chat.

"Levi Hamilton, I haven't seen you in years. How's it going?" Tim said as the two former co-workers shook hands.

"Good to see you again, Tim. It's been awhile."

"Yeah, I think it was at my going-away party when I got bounced from the station in Cleveland."

"Yes, but you landed on your feet. Just think: You'll be the White House press secretary in a few months."

"Yeah, that is a little scary. Hey, last I heard you were working for ECCN. Aren't you a bit far from home?"

"Yes, I am, I'm on special assignment."

"Are you here for Jeff?"

"Yes, we want to do a couple of one-on-one interviews with Jeff Burris and Eddie Blanton."

"That's great, we'll take any air-time we can get. But may I ask why you guys want to talk to both of them?"

"My superiors think America needs to know more about all of the candidates. So I've been assigned the task of securing one-hour commitments from both of the Constitution Party nominees."

"And you flew to Detroit, just for that?"

"Yes."

"Sounds like this came from way up the food chain."

"It came directly from the top. The network president wants us to be the number-one source of election information on the East Coast. If we can do it, we stand a better chance of catching up to CNN, MSNBC and FOX News. They kill us in the ratings and, if we can quote, 'own this story,' it would give us some ratings momentum," Levi said using the line he had rehearsed.

"Tell me Madge didn't say, 'we've got to own this story,'" Tim asked with a smile.

"You know she did; that's why you're smiling."

"When do you want to do the interviews?"

"How about Labor Day?"

"Tape, or live?"

"Live."

"Let me get with Jeff, and I'll let you know."

"Thanks."

Having accomplished the first part of his mission, Levi slipped out of the room and headed back to the airport. Now all he had to do was fly back to New York and convince Madge Thratton, Vice President and General Manager of ECCN, that the interviews were a good idea. He had used her often-repeated mantra "own the story" because he knew that Tim, as well as anyone else in the broadcast industry, would be familiar with it. Madge was not often swayed, but the odds were in Levi's favor, and this was story that he had to "own."

When his plane landed shortly after midnight, he took a taxi back to the hospital. From the moment they re-united at sea Olivia had become the focus of his life and he wanted to be there the moment she awakened. When he arrived at the hospital, Brad was asleep in the chair next to Jessica. Olivia, still on life-support, lay motionless. Neither woman's health had shown any marked improvement so Levi went home to his upper west side apartment.

He knew that he would need to be well informed and armed for battle when he went into Madge Thratton's office on Monday morning, so he spent that weekend at work in the network's research department reading archived articles and surfing the Internet for information on the two nominees.

The fact that they were both well known with lengthy political careers created volumes of information, and Levi read every tidbit he could find on the two men. The veteran newsman created chronological timelines and traced their lives backward going so far as to peer into their childhood. He read everything from their grade school transcripts, to their law school applications, to their marriage licenses.

Searching through the maze of public documents and utilizing his own personal contacts he was able re-construct their lives from the day they were born. However, it was a search of archived college newspapers that led his investigation to an unexpected revelation. From what he could discern no one else had made this connection. In his attempt to distract himself from a painful personal situation Levi Hamilton had unearthed information that could affect the race for the highest office in the land.

*   *   *

After a working weekend spent verifying the information he had uncovered, that Monday morning Levi stopped at the hospital to check on Jessica and Olivia. Olivia lay peacefully while the machines continued to beep and blink as they monitored her condition. He kissed her cheek as he always did. He paused for a minute, waiting for a response, but there was none. He spoke briefly with Jessica before leaving for work. He was on his way to the most important meeting of his career.

"Hi, I need to speak with Madge on an urgent matter," Levi said to the secretary.

"Of course Mr. Hamilton. I'll see if she can see you now," the woman said as she buzzed her boss' office.

"Send him in," Madge Thratton's voice said through the tiny speaker on the secretary's desk.

"Thank you," Levi said as he took a deep breath and walked toward the door.

"Good morning, Madge," Levi said when he walked through the door.

"Morning, yourself. I haven't had a chance to chat with you in ages," she said as she walked around her desk and motioned toward two chairs sitting next to a small round coffee table. "Have a seat and tell me what brings you up here this morning."

"Well, I was on vacation last week," he began.

"Yes, Ned told me he forced you to take some time off but you came back early."

Levi smiled. Although her office door was always closed, the veteran newswoman, who had covered every big story from the Apollo13 tragedy to the death of Princess Di, knew everything that went on at the network. It seemed that nothing ever got past her and many employees speculated that she had microphones and cameras hidden throughout the building.

"Yes, ma'am, he did. I took a cruise, but cut it short because I got word that a project I was working on had come to fruition."

"Okay, you've got my attention. Pitch me?"

"One-hour interviews with Jeff Burris and Eddie Blanton. Live or live-to-tape. The campaign manager is an old friend of mine from my days back in Cleveland. We've spoken and it's a go, pending your approval."

"Two separate interviews, one hour each?"

"Yes."

"I take it that's why you spent the weekend in research?"

"Yes," Levi answered, wondering how she knew he was there.

"What do you have in mind for a tentative air date?"

"Labor Day."

"You're cutting it close, that's only a week away."

"I'm ready."

"I need something more. I'm not going to put these guys on the air for a one-hour unpaid political ad. Tell me what you've found or it's a 'no go'."

"Just between you and me?"

"Do you really have to ask?"

"One of the nominees has a secret."

"Now you're speaking my language. Tell me more?"

Levi told Madge Thratton the full story of what he'd uncovered. As he expected she was delighted with the revelation and ready to forge ahead full-speed.

"Are you prepared to ask the nominee about this on the air?"

"Yes, I am."

"If we do these interviews, we're going to aggressively promote them in all forms of media. Are you comfortable with that?"

"Whatever you decide. I trust your judgment."

"Levi, this will put ECCN on the map. We've been trying to find a way to distinguish ourselves from the other cable news networks, and now you've done it. You've got a full green light on this project. Ned will give you anything you need to make these interviews the biggest and best shows we've ever done."

"Thank you, Madge."

"No, Levi. Thank *you* for coming to me with this opportunity."

"Just doing my job, Madge."

Ignoring his self-deprecation she stated the plan she'd just formulated. "We'll do live interviews, complete with e-mail questions from viewers. We'll follow each interview with a one-hour town hall meeting. Our numbers are weak in Tampa and in Boston, so we'll do the town hall meetings in those two cities. That will give us four hours of coverage."

"Well, I'd better get to work," he said as he prepared to leave.

"Yes, you'd better. Oh, one more thing, Levi," she added.

"Yes, Madge."

"The next time you want to secure a presidential candidate interview, get my approval first. I could have gotten this for you without that trip to Detroit."

For the next week Levi spent every waking hour preparing for the interviews. He organized his notes in his laptop and carried it with him wherever he went. He normally worked from 2 p.m. until 11 p.m., but this week his routine changed. He would start his day with a visit to the hospital and arrive in his office by 10 a.m. where he would study his notes until late afternoon when he would break for lunch. After that he would prepare to anchor the nightly news block. And each day ended with another hospital visit.

The week breezed by and, just as Madge Thratton had promised, the network purchased billboards and an extensive radio and television campaign to promote the upcoming interviews. Normally the advertising blitz would have brought joy to Levi's heart and filled him with pride. Knowing that the network had enough confidence to promote his work brought him little solace when he thought of Olivia in the hospital.

13

The sounds of the ventilator pumping air into the lungs of one comatose woman and the constant whirl of the dialysis machine filtering the blood of her daughter filled ICU Suite #4 at Manhattan General Hospital. It had been ten days since Olivia's return from Miami. Ashen and gaunt she lay prone as Jessica read to her.

"Mom, it looks like Jennifer Lopez is at it again. Sources tell People the Puerto Rican diva is about to stroll down the aisle for the fourth time. This time she's going to marry some goofy TV weather guy from Indiana. How crazy is that?" Jessica said.

Each day she read to her mother. They both enjoyed Hollywood gossip, so People magazine and Entertainment Weekly were must-reads, along with a healthy dose of tabloids. Looking forward to the moment Olivia awakened, Jessica spoke to her often. She refused to believe that her mother was gone forever.

"Newsweek says that Levi is going to interview the two guys running against President Greenlee on ECCN. Right now they are trailing in the polls by six percent, so it doesn't look good for them."

"Good afternoon, Jessica," Dr. Orland said as he entered the room. "How are you feeling today?"

"Hi, Dr. Orland. I'm feeling okay, just a little weak, that's all. I was reading to Mom."

"I think it's good that you do that. We find many times that coma victims are able to hear what's going on around them even though they are unable to answer, and sometimes give full accounts after they awaken."

"I hope it's soon."

"So do I, Jessica. I have someone for you to meet. Are you up to it?"

"Sure."

"Good," he said before opening the door and motioning for his colleague to join him. "This is Dr. Marklewood, the top transplant nephrologist on the East Coast, and he'd like to talk to you."

"Hello, Dr. Marklewood. I'd get up, but as you can see, they've got me strapped in pretty good."

The portly physician entered the room cleaning his glasses and took a seat near her bedside. Meanwhile Dr. Orland walked over to the next bed to examine Olivia.

"Well, we have to make sure you're not out running marathons or anything like that," Dr. Marklewood said.

"Believe me doctor running was never my strong suit. Even before the accident."

"Well, my goal is to have you up and close to running as soon as possible."

"Sounds good to me."

"I just wanted to go over your case with you and discuss the transplant procedure."

"Yes?"

"Your condition is stable and your baby is fine. It appears she has suffered no ill effects from the accident or from the subsequent medical treatment. I believe you will be able to carry your baby to full-term as long as you remain hospitalized."

"Yes, I know that."

"However, it appears that your kidney damage is severe and that a transplant is your only hope."

"I thought that with dialysis and with time, I would see improvement?"

"I'm afraid that's not going to happen. The muscle damage you sustained in your auto accident caused the release of a large amount of toxic proteins. That has caused end-stage renal failure."

"So, what's next?"

"First we wait for a donor. Once we achieve a match, we take the baby by Caesarian, then do the transplant immediately. You'll be hospitalized for about two weeks following that."

"What about the baby?"

"Naturally the closer she gets to full-term the better; but, depending on her weight and development, the two of you should be ready to go home at about the same time."

"What about Mom?"

"When she wakes up, it will take a week or two for her to regain her strength. Still, I would advise against performing surgery on her so soon after her trauma."

"Don't worry doctor, I can hang in there, and so can Mom. Sagamore women are a lot tougher than you might think."

"From what I've seen so far. I believe it; and on that note, I'll let you get some rest," Dr. Marklewood said before leaving.

Dr. Orland finished examining Olivia and gave Jessica an update on her mother's condition.

"Her best motor response has improved. Her Glasgow Coma Score is up to seven. Keep reading to her, Jessica. I'm sure it's helping," Dr. Orland said as his pager went off. "I'm sorry, I have to go. I'll send in the physical therapist."

The third physician of the day entered the room and began to stretch and flex Olivia's limbs and joints. The daily exercise regimen was necessary to maintain strength in her arms and legs and to prevent muscular atrophy. A few hours later, Levi arrived for his nightly visit. The interviews with the nominees were scheduled for the next day and he had been working around the clock to prepare for the programs.

"Good evening, Levi, you look a little tired," Jessica said as the dialysis machine filtering her blood hummed on.

"Hi, Jessica. How are you feeling?"

"I'm fine, how about you?"

"I'm okay."

"Where's Brad?"

"I forced him to go home and get some rest. I told him if he came in here today, I'd get out of this bed and kick his butt."

"Well, then, I don't blame him for staying away."

"He'd better, if he knows what's good for him."

"Jessica, we need to talk."

"Is there something wrong?"

"Not really, but there is something you need to know."

"What is it?" Jessica asked softly.

Levi hesitated as his mind muddled over what he had planned to say. He opened his mouth and looked at Jessica. Normally a very articulate man, the words he'd rehearsed failed him. Instead he spoke from his heart.

"Jessica, you, your baby and your mother are going to come through this together and I'm going to do everything I can to help you. I just hope you'll understand that I have only your best interests in mind. Please know that."

"I know you care for us and I can't thank you enough for being here for mom and me."

"Well, I've got a long day tomorrow and I'm a little tired so I'll go and let you get some rest."

"All right, I'll see you tomorrow."

"Good night," he said before kissing her on the forehead and leaving.

Jessica sat quietly for a few minutes and gently rubbed her tummy. "You hear that, Mom? All three of us are going to be okay," Jessica said before falling asleep.

14

Led by an eight-member police escort that parted the traffic ahead, the long black limousine splashed through large puddles of water as it cruised through the crowded streets of Manhattan. Inside were the two Constitution Party nominees, their campaign manager and three advisers.

A steady shower of raindrops pelted the car as it arrived at the Upper East Side street-level studios of the East Coast Cable News Network. In spite of the downpour a throng of no less than three hundred supporters, many waving signs and chanting, shouting, "It's time for a change! Vote Burris/Blanton!"

The two candidates climbed out of the car and acknowledged the crowd with a brief wave before security ushered them into the building. They entered the large glass doors and were quickly led to the green room where they would huddle for next half hour. It would be the last strategy session before the broadcast began.

"Thanks for letting us have this interview, Governor. It will do a great deal for our network," Ned Madigan said graciously as he greeted the candidate and led him to the set.

"Thank you for allowing me the opportunity to speak to your viewers. They can do a great deal for our cause with their vote," Jeff Burris said.

"Here you are, sir. You can just clip this to your tie," the floor director said as she handed the nominee a wireless microphone.

Jeff clipped on the microphone and sat still while what seemed like five pounds of powder was dusted on his face. Technicians around the room adjusted lights, tested microphones and delivered scripts while he watched. Ned Madigan stood quietly in the corner. His experienced eyes darted back and forth as he watched the carefully choreographed dance routine. Levi Hamilton walked in and Ned whispered a few words to him, patting him on the back.

"Governor Burris, thank you so much for agreeing to chat with us tonight," Levi said.

"It's a pleasure, Levi. Besides, I know you and Tim go way back," Jeff said.

"Yes, we worked together years ago," Levi said making small talk to put his guest at ease.

"Five minutes until air time," the floor director said as she set a platter with a pitcher of water and two glasses on the table between the two men.

"Thanks Jeanie," Levi said.

"Levi, do you need anything else?" Ned Madigan asked.

"Nope, we're good to go."

"Have a good show. Good luck, Governor," Ned said before leaving the studio to take his position in the control room.

"Camera one, get a close-up on Levi. Camera two, let me have a two shot, and camera three close-up on the governor," the director barked from the control room.

"Here comes the open," Jeanie said. In five, four, three, two, one."

"Live from our network studios in New York, an East Coast Cable News Election Special, with your host, Levi Hamilton," the announcer's voice boomed over the rich symphonic arrangement.

"Ready, camera one. Cue Levi," the director said as the floor director waved her hand, relaying the command.

"Good evening, and welcome to a special commercial-free program. Joining us tonight in a one-on-one interview is

Constitution Party presidential nominee Jefferson Burris, governor of California. Thank you for joining us tonight, Governor," Levi began.

"Thank you, Levi, I'm honored to be here and grateful for the opportunity to share my vision for this great country, but please call me Jeff. The only people who call me Jefferson are my wife and my mom and usually it's because I'm in trouble."

"Of course, Governor. Jeff it is."

"Not only are we going to get to hear the governor's position on the issues that define this campaign, but he will also answer questions from you tonight. All you have to do is send an email to election@eccn.com. We will show this address to you at various times throughout our conversation tonight. Now, immediately following this program will be an hour-long town hall meeting from Boston, broadcast live on the air. Here's a look at the scene at historic Churchill Hall on the campus of Northeastern University, where the town hall meeting will take place. Our coverage there will be anchored by campaign correspondent Natalie Jamison, and we'll talk to her later in this program."

The interview began with the planned questions about the issues that had defined the campaign. A rather benign exchange led Levi to shift to a more controversial topic.

"Mr. Burris, as Governor of California you've taken an aggressive, some say excessive, approach to fighting terrorism. Explain your position?"

"Well, Levi, we are the most populous state in the nation and as such, we make a very attractive target for those who want to highlight their cause. With that in mind I don't think it's possible to be too aggressive. Under my administration we've instituted stricter policies in all public venues. That has caused some inconveniences, but so far we've been able to prevent major attacks on our citizens. Plus, next to New York City and Washington, D.C., Los Angeles is the third most frequent U.S. destination for international travelers, making it a likely entry point for terrorists. As President, I will continue to strengthen our efforts here at home and across the world to prevent terror attacks," the candidate said, exactly as he had been coached by Roderick Schilling.

"Speaking of international efforts, how would you position the U.S. in relation to the Middle East?"

"Firmly. I think we've gone further than we should have to placate those who differ with us philosophically. The time has come to stand strong and let the chips fall where they may."

The tenor of his answer took Levi by surprise and he knew he was on to something. "So are you saying you would use force if necessary?"

"Yes. I will use all avenues to protect our shores and our interests. If it comes to force, I will make sure we act swiftly and appropriately."

"Does that mean that you would authorize retaliatory strikes?"

"Yes, it does. I would authorize any and all military measures. I believe in fighting force with a stronger force."

The interview continued with Levi firing questions and follow-ups and with Jeff Burris projecting a tough-as-nails, take-no-prisoners, persona. The program continued with Levi conducting a short question-and-answer session with Natalie Jamison in Boston and then back to Burris with more questions. The show was going along smoothly. Ned had not said a word to Levi through his earpiece, and the show moved on to the e-mail segment.

"Now, Governor, let's answer some viewer e-mail."

"Sure."

"This one comes to us from Theo Daniels of Fishers, Indiana. How do you plan to reign in government spending and maintain a balanced budget?"

"Well, Theo. I plan to use the same measures you use at home. I'm going to watch spending carefully. I think Washington insiders are out of touch with Middle America. Frankly, I'm not going to be afraid to reallocate funds to areas where they could be more useful. I know the government already takes a large enough tax bite, and I don't plan to change that."

"So, Governor, are you saying that you won't raise taxes?"

"Years ago a presidential candidate made the guarantee of no new taxes. What he should have said, is no new taxes that aren't vital to the nation's economic survival," Jeff Burris said, deftly avoiding making a fiscal guarantee.

"Here's another e-mail," Levi began. "Sandy Allstott of Beaumont, Texas writes: What is your position on integrity and family values?"

"Sandy," the candidate said, staring confidently into camera three, "I hold integrity and family values as the keystone of my political and personal philosophy. I have always put my family first and have tried to live a life above reproach and free of scandal. My administration will be one that our nation can be proud of. We won't cut corners or engage in shady politics, either before we are elected, or after we're inaugurated in January. Eddie Blanton and I are two honest men with nothing to hide."

As the allotted hour neared its end, Levi allowed the candidate to summarize.

"We're almost out of time, Governor, so I'll let you have the last word."

"To the voters of America, I say, look at my record. I come from humble beginnings. I was born in Philadelphia and raised in California in the small farm community of Modesto. I've always been a champion of working-class people. Before I entered the political arena I won the largest class action lawsuit in California history. As attorney general, I increased the state's conviction rate amongst frequent offenders. As governor I have balanced the budget of the largest state in the union and all the while kept social services high and the crime rate lower than it was under my predecessor. These qualities make me uniquely qualified to run this country."

"Thank you, Governor Burris, and good luck in November," Levi said as the two men shook hands before he turned to camera one. "Thank you for watching our Election Special. Stay tuned to ECCN. Up next we'll have a town hall meeting live from Boston, followed by one hour live interview with vice presidential candidate, Ohio Senator Eddie Blanton."

The credits rolled and the show close played as Levi and Jeff exchanged pleasantries. The show ended and the town meeting began. Tim Reynolds quickly whisked the governor away so that they could watch the town hall meeting and gauge public feedback. Levi had a few minutes before prepping for his next interview and he decided to call the hospital.

"Hi, Brad, this is Levi. How are Olivia and Jessica?"

"Not good. Not good at all."

"What happened?" Levi asked.

Before he heard an answer he said a silent prayer. His worst thought was that Olivia had died while he was away. Brad's words shook him.

"Levi," Brad said. "I know you have a lot going on tonight and I hate to be the one to tell you this, but Olivia's condition has taken a serious turn for the worse. She had another episode and her GCS dropped to a five. We don't know if she is going to last much longer."

"What happened?" Levi was frantic now.

"Jessica was reading to her and she spiked. When she calmed down, she stopped breathing. She's resting comfortably now."

"Oh, God. How is Jessica?"

"She's pretty upset."

"I'm sure she is. Tell her I'll stop by and see her right after the broadcast. In the meantime, you hold down the fort for me."

"I will."

Levi was devastated. On the biggest night of his career, his new reason for living lay barely alive. He had clung to the belief that Olivia would recover and that they would be together. Now the light at the end of the tunnel was down to a flicker. He refused to give up hope, but he knew now that the possibility of Olivia being a kidney donor for Jessica was over. Levi had prepared for the worst and he knew he would now be forced to ask some very tough questions.

The town hall meeting continued and the crowd response was largely positive. Levi reviewed his notes and prepared for the next interview. Having endured the media circus of Super Bowl week, Eddie Blanton was no stranger to network interviews. He arrived and casually sat, waiting for the program to begin.

The show open rolled and Levi did the introduction, this time mentioning that the live town hall meeting immediately following the hour-long interview would be held in Tampa. He fought hard to control his emotions as he prepared to ask the questions that would alter the perception of one of the nation's sports heroes, but with Jessica's life hanging in the balance - it was a small price to pay.

"Senator Blanton, most of America knows you as a pro football Hall of Famer, and a collegiate and professional champion. You could have made a lot more money as a broadcaster, but you chose politics. Why did you make that choice?"

"Football came naturally to me. From the time I was in the peewee league, it was fun and I was good at it. The more I played, the better I got. After a while, I realized that I was better at football than anything else. Like most young boys who grew up on the East Coast I had pictures of Joe Namath and Johnny Unitas on my bedroom wall. They were my heroes and I wanted to be like them. After my football career was over I moved back to Columbus, Ohio. I had gone to Ohio State and my wife is from there. I always wanted to give back something to the community, so after I finished law school I ran for mayor. Most people thought I ran for election because I was a popular athlete who missed the limelight, but when they took time to listen to me, they found out that I had some good ideas on how to make mid-Ohio a better place to live."

"What has been your biggest political accomplishment so far?"

"As a mayor I'd have to say our restructuring of the Columbus city school system. We took an organization that was not functioning efficiently and made it a model educational program for the rest of the nation to emulate. As a senator I've been part of legislation that will rebuild Ohio's steel industry, and create and maintain more than eleven thousand jobs."

Levi had spent a half-hour putting the vice-presidential candidate at ease when Ned Madigan spoke to him through the IFB in his ear for the first time that evening.

"Enough small talk, Levi, let's move on to the good stuff," he said.

"Senator, earlier tonight a viewer wrote in to ask Governor Burris about his position on integrity and family values. I'll now offer you the chance to expound on those topics."

"I'd be happy to. I think that too often politicians talk a good game about integrity but they don't always stand up to scrutiny. As a football player I always tried to be a role model and live a life that my family and I could be proud of. My family values have always been my guiding barometer. I could have continued to play pro football, but I didn't want to move my wife and son around the country just so I could hang on in the league for a few more years. So I moved back to Columbus to allow my son to grow up near his grandma and grandpa."

"Senator you have one son, is that correct?"

"Yes, Lindsay and I only have one child and we are very proud of him."

"You never had any other children?"

"No."

"Senator, do you know a woman by the name of Olivia Cavillian Sagamore?"

"No, I don't think I do."

"Are you sure?" Levi asked looking him directly in the eye.

"No, the name doesn't ring a bell at all," Eddie Blanton answered.

"Would you take a look at this?" Levi asked as he handed Eddie a sheet of paper.

"Camera one, give me a wider shot on the senator and zoom in slowly," the director said into the microphone.

"It looks like a birth certificate from about thirty or thirty-five years ago," the senator said as he took time to carefully examine the document.

"It's the birth certificate of Jessica LeAnn Sagamore. Would you please read the names of the parents?"

"The mother is Olivia Sagamore, and the father is," Eddie paused, not believing his eyes.

"The father's name is listed as Edward Keith Blanton, is it not?" Levi asked.

"I don't have any idea what this is all about or where you're going with this," said the puzzled candidate.

Eddie looked over to Tim Reynolds. The Burris/Blanton campaign manager was angry and confused. He had known Levi for decades and had never seen him use such underhanded tactics. He would be sure to discuss this ambush with Madge Thratton.

"Senator Blanton, we have learned that this birth certificate is authentic."

Suddenly not as relaxed as he had been moments ago Blanton blurted, "Mr. Hamilton, I have been happily married for over thirty-one years. I have no idea who this woman is and I can assure you I am not the father of her child. I don't know where you got this phony birth certificate but I guarantee you it has nothing to do with me. Obviously our opponents are more worried about us that they want anyone to believe."

"With all due respect senator, these questions are based on my own research. In an article in the campus newspaper dated April 4, 1970, you stated that you had spent the previous week enjoying spring break in New York with your family and your girlfriend. Is that not true?"

"Yes."

"Were you romantically involved with Olivia Cavillian during that time?"

"I think so," the senator said, his memory now refreshed by Levi's queries.

"Was she your girlfriend at that time?"

"Yes."

"Was she your only girlfriend at that time?"

"Yes."

"Did you father a child with Olivia Cavillian?"

"No."

"Is that not your full name listed there as the father?"

"Yes, that's my name. But I'm not the father of that child."

"Senator Blanton, are you telling the American people that you have a thirty-four year old child that you know nothing about?"

Blanton answered emphatically, delivering the sound bite that would haunt him for days.

"I'm saying that this woman, whoever she is, is not my daughter," the candidate clearly stated.

Ned Madigan smiled a wide grin in the control room. Madge Thratton stood in the center of the newsroom, her eyes locked on the fifty-four inch television screen in front of her. The rest of her staff was engrossed in the program. Charged by Blanton's denials Levi Hamilton forged on.

"Senator, not only is this woman your daughter but right now she is in end-stage renal failure at Manhattan General. She needs a kidney transplant and you may be the only person who can save her life."

"What are you talking about? I don't know this woman and she is not my daughter. If she needs a donor, why doesn't her mother provide what she needs?" Blanton asked, giving Levi the opening he had been waiting for.

"Well, Senator, the mother is a direct HLA match, but the problem is that she's in a hospital bed next to her daughter. She's been in a coma for almost two weeks. According to her doctors her condition worsened earlier tonight and she is near death. So, Senator, the only person who can save your daughter's life is you." Levi said.

"That's it. This interview is over," Tim Reynolds said as he barged onto the set. "Let's go, Senator Blanton, I'm not going to let you be subjected to this. My God, Levi I can't believe you would stoop so low."

"Wait. Before you go I have one more question."

"Save it!" Tim shouted.

"Senator, your daughter is seven months pregnant. If you don't help her, she and her baby, your grandchild - will die. What do you have to say to that?" Levi shouted as the two angry men bolted from the studio.

The hour-long interview still had fifteen minutes to go before the town hall meeting was scheduled to begin. The audience gathered in the conference room at the Tampa Bay Convention Center was stunned and began chattering nervously. In the ECCN control room, Ned Madigan sprang into action while Madge Thratton watched intently. The fact that the normally cool-under-pressure senator tore out of the studio prematurely would play well on evening newscasts across the nation for days, giving her network publicity and extra credibility.

"Levi, we're going to replay the last few minutes of the interview. The tape will be ready in less than a minute, so you need to fill," Ned instructed seconds after the senator walked out.

Not skipping a beat, Levi began speaking. "You've been watching what was scheduled as an hour long interview with Ohio Senator Eddie Blanton. This reporter uncovered, and verified, some sensitive information about his past and was sharing it with the vice presidential nominee when he chose to hastily end the interview. Now, we are still going to Tampa for a town hall meeting at the top of the hour, and we'll see how those gathered in the convention center feel about tonight's revelations and the candidate's reaction. If you'd like to let us know how you feel, send us an e-mail at election@eccn.com."

The tape room technicians had scrambled to rewind tape to the exact point where Levi began to confront the candidate.

"The tape is ready, Levi," Ned said.

"Here's a look back at what just transpired a few moments ago," Levi said as the tape began.

"Levi, we've got quite a bit of time to fill. I want you to solicit more e-mail on the latest revelation of the campaign. Then we're going to toss to Tampa for some crowd reaction. That will buy us some time to accumulate some e-mail on the server. We'll re-rack the end of the interview and then go back to Florida for the town meeting," Ned Madigan said into the IFB.

"I gotcha, Ned, glad to have you along for the ride."

The veteran newsman shrugged his normally drooping shoulders and said, "Hey, it's what we live for, right?"

The pro-Burris/Blanton crowd outside the studios, wildly enthusiastic and larger before - was now smaller and subdued. The driving rain had soaked their spirits, faded their signs and Eddie Blanton's revelation had dashed their hopes of a November victory. In the shadow of the jumbo screen their numbers had diminished to fewer than fifty as they stood watching the remainder of the news program.

Rivulets of rain ran down the large glass windows outside the studios, the water disappearing as it washed down nearby drains. While inside, Levi Hamilton began to ad-lib.

"We have just revealed some sensitive information involving Ohio senator and vice-presidential candidate Eddie Blanton and his illegitimate child," he began. "When we shared the information with the senator he became outraged, terminated our interview, and left the building. So we have a little extra time and we'd like to hear from you. Send us an e-mail to the address on your screen and we'll air your views. Before we get to that, let's go to Leslie Sandoval in Tampa. Leslie, what is the mood there in the convention center?"

"Well, Levi, the mood here is a mixture of anger and disappointment," she began.

*   *   *

Jeff Burris watched the report from Tampa in his hotel room near the ECCN studios. He was livid that Eddie Blanton had apparently destroyed his chances of getting elected, and he made an angry phone call to Minnesota.

"Well, Schilling, I hope you're happy. I guess you didn't do a good enough job of checking out your boy. Now the party has no chance unless we dump him off the ticket," Jeff sneered.

"Shut up, Jeff, and listen to me! Of course we didn't know anything about this. First, we have to verify that it's true. I've got people working on that right now. If it is, then we'll find a way to spin it. In the meantime, you make yourself scarce. I don't want to see you anywhere in front of a microphone or camera until I say so," the party chairman said.

"I can't just disappear. I'm running for president of the United States in case you may have forgotten that fact. There is nowhere I can hide."

"Don't be so melodramatic, Jeff. Find Eddie, and the two of you get on his plane and fly to Duluth. I'll meet you there. I've got the perfect place for you two to lay low for a couple of days while this thing blows over."

      *   *   *

As Leslie gave her report from Tampa, Levi took a sip of water and relaxed as thousands of e-mail messages poured in from across the nation. After her report ended, Levi presented a sampling of viewer e-mail. The responses ranged from surprise over the revelation to disgust with Levi for disclosing the information.

For a fourth time, the final minutes of the interview were shown before the program ended and the town hall meeting began in Tampa. Relieved that the broadcast was over, Levi went in for his scheduled post-production meeting with Ned and Madge. When he walked into the newsroom the thirty-member staff stood and applauded.

"Good work, Levi. You handled yourself well when he walked out," Ned said.

"Everyone, may I have your attention please!" Madge said, raising her voice over the noise, and waiting for complete silence before speaking. "Levi Hamilton came back early from vacation and flew to Detroit out of his own pocket to get the two interviews we aired tonight. Though, I'm sure he'll expense the trip."

Levi grinned and nodded in agreement, while laughter ricocheted across the newsroom.

"Enterprising journalism," Madge began again. "I've been preaching the philosophy for years and tonight we saw its power in action. We owe Levi a huge thank-you and a pat on the back for his efforts. We have been trying for almost two decades to accomplish what we finally achieved tonight. I'm especially glad that one of the old dogs, who, like me, was here from day one, was able to put us over the top. Tonight, East Coast Cable News took a quantum leap ahead. MSNBC, CNN, FOX News and the four over-the-air networks have called requesting video feed. In our seventeen-year history that has never happened. For the first time we have exclusive rights to the biggest story of the year. Thank you all for your hard work tonight. And Levi, thank you for bringing this story to us."

"Thanks, Madge. I couldn't have done a program like the one we did tonight without Ned in the booth and without your support. Thanks to all of you, and let's hope that this is just the beginning of a new era of success for ECCN," Levi said.

After a few minutes receiving congratulations from his co-workers, Levi slipped out of the room and into a taxi. A half-hour later he arrived at Manhattan General where a hoard of media types gathered at the front door. Not wanting to attract attention, Levi slipped in through the emergency entrance and went up to see Jessica and Olivia. The hospital had posted a security guard at the door, but Levi was allowed to enter. He walked in fully prepared for the conversation he would now have with Jessica. She was propped on the same pillows where she'd sat the night before.

"Hi Brad, how is Jessica?" Levi whispered.

"I'm fine," she said curtly. "We need to talk."

"You first, or me?" Levi asked.

She answered, "You."

Levi took a seat and began to speak. Brad held Jessica's hand as Levi repeated the story Olivia had told him on the cruise in the Caribbean. He showed Jessica the newspaper article where Eddie stated that he was in New York during the time she was conceived. Her skepticism was obvious until Levi showed her the official birth certificate listing Olivia Cavillian and Edward Blanton as her parents.

"If Parker Sagamore was married to my mother when I was born, then why was he not listed as my father? And why have I never seen this document until now?"

"I don't know Jessica, those are questions only your mom can answer," Levi replied.

Except for the sound of the machines and monitors connected to the two women the room was silent until Jessica spoke again.

"By the way, nice job tonight Levi."

"Thanks Jessica. That means a lot coming from you. Do you understand," he began.

She interrupted, "I understand why you told him about me. You want him to give me a kidney because you know Mom can't be a donor, and if he doesn't help me, I won't make it."

"Honey, don't say that," Brad said.

"It's okay, Brad. I know what's going on, and I'm okay with it. Levi, go over and talk to Mom. Be strong for her; she needs you right now. I have a lot on my mind and I need to get some sleep. We'll talk tomorrow."

"Sleep well," Levi said.

Levi walked over to Olivia's bed and took a seat. He held her hand and stroked her hair as he had on the cruise ship while he told her about the two interviews. Her only movement was her chest going up and down as the ventilator breathed for her. Levi sat with her for more than an hour before going home.

The next day the network switchboard was jammed with angry callers. The feedback was the largest single subject response in the network's history. Levi expected the negative backlash. Not since the Connie Chung interview with Newt Gingrich's mother had an interviewer been so vehemently vilified for simply asking questions. His computer was jammed with e-mail - some hateful, denouncing his tactics - and some in praise of his removing the mask of virtue from yet another deceitful politician.

15

The revelation that Eddie Blanton had fathered an out-of-wedlock child was the top story on all the Tuesday network newscasts and word of the emotional outburst at the untimely ending of the interview was the top subject on radio talk shows coast to coast. ECCN retained its exclusive rights to the abrupt ending to the one-on-one interview, and aired the video numerous times throughout the day.

A special rebroadcast of both interviews aired at 7 p.m., followed by a roundtable of political pundits discussing the implications of the scandal. The encore showing of the programs drew even higher ratings than the original.

"I can't believe you didn't know this woman existed," Jeff Burris said as he, Eddie Blanton, and Roderick Schilling watched the re-broadcast from their hidden location in rural Minnesota.

"We still don't know for sure if this is on the level," Eddie said.

"The hell we don't! It's been confirmed by my staff. That woman is your daughter and she's eight months pregnant. She had a car accident and her kidneys are damaged beyond repair. She needs a transplant and her only match is her mother, but the mother's in a coma and can't be a donor. The only thing that will save your ass is if they both die!" Roderick snorted.

"How likely is that?" Jeff asked.

"The mother definitely won't make it. The moment they unplug the ventilator, she's as good as dead. The daughter needs a transplant within the next few weeks. She's on the donor list, so it's a waiting game for her."

"What if I acknowledge paternity and donate a kidney?" Eddie asked.

"You'd have to admit that she's your daughter which would be political suicide. Even if she is your daughter, if you're not a direct match you've ruined your political career for nothing," Jeff said.

"He's right. You can't admit paternity. If you do, we can kiss this election goodbye," Roderick said. "I'm trying to get her moved up on the donor list. Once she gets a kidney, no one will care if you're her father or not."

"How can you get her moved up on the donor list?" Eddie asked.

"Don't you worry about that. For your sake, just hope he gets it taken care of in time," Jeff interjected.

"Wait a minute, you two. We've got a bigger problem," Roderick Schilling said as he read the letter that had just been faxed to him.

Since his nomination at the convention, Jeff Burris had openly challenged President Greenlee and his running mate to a debate. A list of places and dates had been previously submitted and now, sensing opportunity, Vice President Matthew Adams had accepted the open challenge for a vice-presidential debate. The date chosen from the list selected by Roderick Schilling and presented by Jeff Burris was September fifteenth, only ten days away. The debate would be held in Chicago.

The Constitution Party was in deep trouble and their only choice was to agree to the contest. Throughout the campaign Jeff Burris had promised to accept any parameters set forth by the incumbent. It was a vow he now regretted when he saw the debate format. Each candidate would give five-minute opening and closing statements, with Blanton speaking first and Adams speaking last. Further stacking the odds against the challenger was the fact that the moderator of the debate would be none other than Levi Hamilton.

Choosing Levi to ask the questions was the Liberty Party's way to ensure that the nation would remember Eddie Blanton's hastily-ended interview upon the revelation of his illegitimate daughter.

16

While the political powwow continued in Minnesota, another heart-to-heart conversation was taking place in New York. While it was possible for her to survive for years on life support, the time had come to have the inevitable conversation about Olivia. Drs. Orland and Marklewood joined Levi, Brad and Jessica to answer two burning questions. What quality of life would Olivia have on the ventilator? And would Jessica save her own life at the expense of her mother's by proceeding with the transplant?

"Jessica, as the only surviving relative, you must make this decision," the hospital chief of staff began.

"We know this will be difficult for you, but we want you to make an informed choice. If you have any questions, we're prepared to answer them for you," Dr. Marklewood said.

"What happens when we turn off the ventilator?" she asked.

"Your mother has lapsed into a deep coma and is ventilator-dependent. Her last EEG showed minimal brain activity."

"So she's not brain dead?"

"No, she's not, but she's very close. In most cases like hers the patient will not survive long once the equipment is turned off. It will be a painless death," he replied.

"It there any chance she could resume breathing on her own?"

"Yes, but in most of these cases, death is imminent."

Tears rolled silently down Jessica's agonized face.

"Brad, Levi, what do you think we should do?" she asked.

"I think you should let her go peacefully," Brad answered.

"She would want you to have the transplant. That way she could live on through you and the baby," Levi added.

"Is there any reason to do anything right now?"

"No. Her condition is stable and you need more time to allow the baby to fully develop. As long as both of you remain as you are right now, there is no reason to move forward. However, if either your condition or hers begins to deteriorate, then we'd need to proceed immediately," Dr. Orland said.

"What would happen then?"

"First we'd move both of you into surgery. Then, we'd disconnect Olivia and allow you to say goodbye. As soon as she was pronounced, one team led by Dr. Orland would harvest the kidney. My team would perform a Caesarian birth and then the kidney transplant. If everything went well you'd be home in a couple of weeks," Dr. Marklewood answered.

"How long can we wait?"

"Jessica, I know that you've been in that bed for twelve days, but another two weeks would be ideal. It would put the baby at thirty-six weeks and I think that would give her enough time," said Dr. Orland.

"That means I've got two weeks to get Mom to wake up. I'm sure I can do it by then," Jessica answered confidently, her face alight with purpose now.

The four men exchanged silent glances, in awe of the confident woman. Their eyes told what their mouths dared not say - only Levi shared her resolve.

For the next ten days Jessica worked herself to the brink of exhaustion trying to reach her mother. She read every page of the New York Times to her each day and the hospital room was filled with pictures of important moments from Olivia's life. Everything from Olivia's childhood school portraits and wedding pictures, to photos of Jessica at birth were displayed. Levi continued to visit daily and took the liberty of smuggling in a portable CD and cassette player so that Jessica could play the tunes he and Olivia had danced to on the cruise.

Their efforts, though well intentioned, were futile. Olivia was unresponsive and her condition remained unchanged.

17

The Windy City was awash in fall colors with the trees in Grant Park dropping the green mask of summer and proudly displaying the golden red, orange and yellow hues of fall. The election was fast approaching and the Liberty Party still led the polls. It would take a strong showing over the next seven weeks if the Burris/Blanton ticket had any hope of unseating the incumbents.

With less than two weeks lead time, Roderick Schilling and Jeff Burris had worked around the clock to prepare Eddie for the most important performance of his life. The three men knew the election hung in the balance and that the odds were against them, so they left nothing to chance. Covering everything from domestic and international affairs to the economy, they worked tirelessly to ensure that Eddie was well versed in all matters of government policy.

As it turned out, Eddie already had a much larger knowledge of issues facing the nation than he had previously shown and was an expert on the economy. His only weakness was on the international scene, and Roderick Schilling was able to tutor him. Eddie proved to be a quick study, and by the end of the training sessions, Jeff Burris had gained a newfound respect for his running mate. Fully prepared to answer any questions that might be thrown his way, Eddie Blanton stood calmly onstage and waited for the debate to begin.

Eddie was not the only one who had spent the past few days cramming. Levi Hamilton had also done his share of reading and searching for information. On the nightly ECCN newscasts, viewer input was solicited and, after sorting through the volumes of e-mail, Levi compiled a list of ten questions from citizens. Combined with the queries he planned to make, all together he had twenty-five questions for the two candidates. With each man allotted three minutes to answer each question, Levi knew he had more than enough content for the program.

"Good evening ladies and gentleman," Levi Hamilton said from the center-stage podium in the Chicago Exposition Hall. "We are coming to you from Chicago and we welcome you to tonight's vice-presidential debate between the incumbent, Vice President Matthew Adams, and the challenger, Ohio Senator Eddie Blanton."

The two men who had spent the last few weeks verbally sparring and jousting met in the middle of the stage, smiled, and cordially shook hands before to moving to their individual battle stations.

"Senator Blanton, you may give your opening statement," Levi said as the event began.

"Thank you, Levi, and thank you, to the citizens of Chicago, for allowing us to be with you this evening. On behalf of the Constitution Party and the great state of Ohio, let me say how honored I am to be here tonight. The last time I was in Chicago, I threw three interceptions and my team got beat 44-27 in a playoff game, so I hope I do much better this time," Eddie Blanton said, acknowledging his underdog status.

The audience erupted in laughter and then applause. A chant of "Eddie! Eddie! Eddie!" filled the room. After playing to the crowd for a bit, he motioned for them to settle down and waited until the room quieted before he spoke again.

"There are some major philosophical differences between the Vice President and me. Tonight, you will get a chance to hear two different visions of which direction America should take. Our country's future is bright, and the Constitution Party is ready to take our great nation to new heights. We've had four years of the Liberty Party's leadership and I'm going to pose a question that every citizen should ask himself now, and again at the end of this debate.

Will you be better off four years from now if the same economic, domestic, and international policies continue? All you have to do is look back at the past four years. That will tell you where the Liberty Party has led the nation. If you take that reflective look and aren't pleased with what you see, then listen carefully tonight. You'll see that you have a chance to choose a fresh path for the nation. I'm going to lay out some bold new initiatives and fresh ideas that will ensure that we maintain our position as the leader of the free world and strongly lead our nation into the new millennium."

The crowd applauded his opening remarks and the former Cleveland quarterback, who had always been a rival to Chicago fans, was for the moment one of their very own. Standing by patiently was Vice President Matthew Adams, ready to pounce on his adversary.

"Vice President Adams, we're ready for your opening statement now," Levi said.

"Thank you, Levi," he said before taking a long pause. "My fellow Americans, tonight is not about whether or not you think things will be better for you four years from now, but about who you think is best prepared to move the country forward. It's about who you think has the character, integrity, experience, and focus. It's about who you trust."

From the beginning of his opening statement it was clear the vice president was going to make tonight's debate about the character of his opponent. Roderick Schilling anticipated this approach and he and Jeff Burris had coached Eddie on how best to defend himself from the attack.

Matthew Adams finished his opening statement and the debate continued. In areas concerning the economy, it was clear that the senator from Ohio was well versed and in many instances more learned that the vice president. Eddie held his own on matters of domestic policy and, while he was weaker on his knowledge of the international front, he made up for it with his passionate stance on social issues.

"It looks like he is going to pull this thing off," Jeff Burris said from the hunting lodge deep in Superior National Forest in northeast Minnesota.

"Don't be so sure, Jeff. We still have fifteen minutes to go, and Adams is waiting for the right opportunity," Roderick Schilling said, never taking his eyes off the television.

"Gentlemen, we only have time for one more question. It comes to us via e-mail from Deborah Kennard of Racine, Wisconsin," Levi said from his center-stage podium. "She asks: as a voter, how much should I consider the character of the individual candidates versus their positions on the issues?"

Jeff and Roderick knew they were dead. Eddie had made it all the way to the final question before the issue they feared most was raised. Roderick had worked with Eddie on an acceptable answer for this question but he knew it was the delivery, not the line, that was important. The two men sat on the edge of their seats in the hunting lodge, and waited while Eddie dealt them their fate.

"As a politician and a voter, I would never vote for any person or any issue that I did not have complete faith in. My character and integrity guide me in everything I do and in every decision I make," Eddie said delivering the line exactly as he had been instructed.

He continued with the answer he had been coached to give, and Jeff and Roderick were pleased with his performance. Next came the vice president's response, and the two men sat motionless with trepidation.

"Mr. Vice President, your response sir?" Levi said.

"I find it odd that my opponent places such a high value on character and integrity. In light of recent events and people in the news, I find it hard to believe that Mr. Blanton has any character or integrity at all, but I guess that is something for voters to decide on November fifth," Matthew Adams said.

"If you have something you want to say, spit it out!" Eddie Blanton interjected angrily.

"Mr. Blanton, you will have a chance to respond to the vice president in your final statement," Levi added.

"Look, it's common knowledge you fathered a child out of wedlock. The woman's mother is in a coma and your daughter is lying in the hospital in need of a kidney transplant, pregnant with your grandchild. You have yet to acknowledge paternity and yet you stand here talking about character and integrity, when it's obvious you lack both qualities," the vice president said.

"Gentlemen, we will take a short break and come back with your closing comments," Levi said before the telecast went to commercial.

"How could he lose it like that?" Jeff asked in disgust.

"It had been building inside him all evening. Let's just hope he sticks to the plan and doesn't have a total meltdown," Roderick said.

After the commercial break the two candidates came back for their final statements. Eddie Blanton had been given a conclusion written for him by the party chairman, but it would go unused on this night. The perennial underdog was about to take a stand he felt he had to take, one that would make or break his political career. It could also wipe away the Constitution Party's chance of winning the election. He had been advised to avoid the issue of Olivia Sagamore and her daughter at all cost. It was advice he would ignore.

"Welcome back to tonight's vice-presidential debate between incumbent Matthew Adams, and challenger Ohio Senator Eddie Blanton. We've had a spirited and informative exchange tonight, and we'll end our program with final remarks from each of the candidates. Senator Blanton will go first," Levi said.

The moment Eddie stared unblinking into the camera and started to speak, Jeff and Roderick knew they had a huge problem on their hands. His steely brown eyes wore the look of confident resolve that had led him to gridiron glory.

"Much has been said and written in the past two weeks about Olivia Sagamore, a woman I met during my collegiate years. Unbeknownst to me until Levi Hamilton informed me, I may have fathered a child with this woman over thirty years ago. This is not something I attempted to hide from public view, or a responsibility I tried to evade, but merely a circumstance I was totally unaware of. I think it would have been more respectful of Mr. Hamilton to have informed me of this situation in private, but he chose to expose what he'd learned, live, on national television. That is something he will have to learn to live with. No one from this woman's family has attempted to contact me to verify whether or not I am truly the father, or if this is a hoax, or even a cruel political dirty trick. Nevertheless, I have never been one to shirk responsibility. I have thought this over carefully during the past few days and I have made an important decision. Tonight I am announcing that I will fly to New York to meet with this young woman and to undergo DNA testing to establish paternity. I understand that she is in need of a kidney transplant and I will also voluntarily submit to any medical tests necessary to determine if I am a compatible donor. If I am a suitable match, regardless of whether I am her father or not, I will give this woman a kidney, immediately. The reason I will do this, is not for public approval, and it is not for your vote on November fifth. I will do this simply because it is the right thing to do."

The ten thousand people in attendance sat in stunned silence. Eighteen years removed from his last snap from center, in a pro football game, Eddie Blanton still had the tools to quiet a hostile crowd on the road. No one expected him to address the allegations so straightforwardly. Expectations were that, as a politician, he would deftly sidestep the issue. Although he was a politician on the outside, Eddie Blanton was still a gridiron gladiator inside, and the gladiator in him always forged ahead into battle.

"Mr. Vice President, you may begin your closing statement," Levi said, his voice echoing much louder in the silent arena.

The vice president fought to regain his composure and stammered through his closing statement. The text he had prepared had been rendered moot by Eddie's announcement. Matthew Adams had never been a quick thinker on his feet and his uneven delivery reflected his poor ad-lib ability. Mercifully for him, time ran out and the event ended as the two adversaries shook hands at center stage.

Inside the hunting lodge in Minnesota the sound of the applauding crowd was momentarily overshadowed by the crash of a glass of thirty-year-old scotch being flung against the wall.

"That cocky son-of-a-bitch, I told him exactly what to say. Now he's ruined everything," Roderick Schilling said.

"I told you we should have kicked him off the ticket," Jeff Burris said.

"Shut up Jeff. There has to be a way out of this, just let me think."

18

Levi flew back to New York, arriving at the hospital just after midnight. It was well past visiting hours but he knew he'd be able to get in for a quick visit. The extra attention from the debate had drawn a few more media types to the hospital's main entrance, so Levi took an alternate route through the emergency room doors.

When he got to the room Olivia lay still as the ventilator kept her alive. Jessica, who had earlier watched the debate and then fallen asleep, was awake but remained quiet, allowing him to speak his mind.

"Olivia, sweetheart, I have something to tell you," he began. "I figured out who Jessica's father is. I know I told you that his identity didn't matter to me and it doesn't, but he has a responsibility to do the right thing for Jessica, so I tracked him down and I confronted him. I refuse to stand by and let your daughter die without a fight. I hope that you understand that I did it for her and for your granddaughter."

"Jessica's father is coming here to give her a kidney, and when you wake up we can all be one big happy family. I know you need your rest, but I just wanted to say goodnight. With all my heart, I love you, Olivia," he said before kissing her forehead and turning to leave.

"Hi, Levi," Jessica said.

"Hi, yourself. What are you doing up so late?"

"The baby, sometimes she wants to be awake when I want to sleep…and she always wins."

"I have a feeling that she is going to win the battles for quite some time.

"Yes, unfortunately you're right," she said with a weak tired smile.

"He's coming here to help you."

"Yeah, I watched the telecast, and I heard you tell Mom about it."

"I'm sorry I was so loud."

"No. You were fine. You did a good thing tonight."

"I don't know about that."

"No, Levi, tonight you saved my life. I'll be sure to tell her about it when she wakes up."

"Think she'll understand?"

"I'm sure she will."

"Thanks, I needed to hear that. Now you get some rest and I'll see you tomorrow," he said before leaving.

Levi left the hospital and went home to try to get some sleep. He knew it would be a difficult task - he hadn't had a good night since Olivia's accident almost a month ago.

Eddie Blanton also had a difficult night ahead. After leaving the Exposition Hall in Chicago he took a limo to Midway Airport. Memories of Olivia, decades old, flashed across his mind as the car motored down the freeway. At the airport he boarded his plane and directed the pilot to fly him to New York City. He ignored the calls on his cell phone from Roderick Schilling and Jeff Burris, only taking the one from his wife.

"Is it true?" she asked.

"Yes."

"How can you be so sure? You've never even met these women."

"Olivia Sagamore was the girl I told you about, the one before you."

"So you're going to destroy everything you've worked for, to help her daughter."

"Yes."

"Just come home and we can talk about it."

"There is nothing to discuss. I'm going to New York."

"Why?'

"To meet my daughter, and save her life."

"Just promise me you won't do anything until you and I talk it over."

"I promise."

It was a promise to his wife that he would later break. It was his duty to donate a kidney and that was exactly what he planned to do. The long black car whisked through traffic and within minutes he was on board the Lear jet he had purchased with the signing bonus from his final pro contract, on his way to New York.

19

At first Dr. Orland was suspicious about the anonymous phone call. He hadn't watched the televised debate and had not yet heard of Eddie Blanton's astonishing announcement. But once he was convinced of the caller's identity and intentions, he reluctantly agreed him on the corner of Central Park South and Avenue of the Americas at 7 p.m., and sneak him into the hospital. It wasn't until he got closer that he realized the man was definitely vice presidential nominee Eddie Blanton. The doctor gave him the extra lab coat hanging in the backseat of his car and handed him a stethoscope.

"If anyone asks, you are Dr. Woodlyn. You're consulting on a pediatric orthopedics case," Dr. Orland said before they entered the hospital, getting a huge thrill despite himself, at the secrecy and intrigue.

The media throng in place since Labor Day had now dwindled to just a few stalwarts. Nevertheless, the two men took the physicians-only, side entrance and boarded the elevator to ICU, where Jessica had been for much of the past month. Standing outside Jessica's room, Dr. Orland gave Eddie the full story.

"Her mother is in the bed next to her. Mrs. Sagamore is a direct HLA match, but she's comatose. The risk of putting her under anesthesia is too great and the chances she would not survive the surgery are high. No responsible surgeon would make that gamble."

"It doesn't sound too promising."

"Jessica is on the list for an organ and we have to hope one comes in soon. It would be better if there was a relative but their whole family is just the two women. There are no siblings and her father is deceased so her only hope for survival is if her mother wakes up, regains her strength, and we perform the transplant."

"What if there was a willing donor?"

"We'd have to do an HLA test and if there was a match, we'd get the consent forms signed, harvest the kidney, and perform the transplant. Complicating matters is that with Jessica's weakened condition we need to have an exact match."

"I know, I'm an exact match," Eddie Blanton said.

"How can you be sure?" Dr. Orland asked.

"I know," Blanton answered, "because I am her father."

The sentence walked confidently out of the senator's mouth and hung heavy in the air. The simple statement, spoken so casually, would profoundly impact many lives, possibly the future course of the nation. The chief of staff and the man who would be vice president stood solemn and let the weight of the confession settle. In their silence the previous words became more voluminous. The gravity of the situation was not lost on the two men as they stared at the woman lying asleep before them.

"I was told that her father died several years ago," the doctor said incredulously.

"He raised her, but I'm the birth father," the crestfallen politician said. "The reports in the media are correct. I'm the only person who can save her, and I have to do it. She's my daughter...How soon can we get started?"

"Will you submit to a DNA test?"

"I'm not here to contest paternity, so I don't need one. Let's just do the other test."

The doctor sat silent as numerous questions raced through his mind. "We have to move quickly, we don't have much time," he said.

"I'm ready to do whatever we need to do."

Dr. Orland quickly drew a blood sample and ran the HLA test himself. The results came back and, six points out of six, it was a complete match, confirming that Eddie Blanton was indeed Jessica's biological father. Only a DNA test could have given a more conclusive result. Next the physician ran a cross-match for antibodies and found none. There was no reason why Eddie's kidney wouldn't be a perfect one for Jessica's transplant. Eddie completed the paperwork agreeing to be a kidney donor and the surgery was scheduled for the following morning.

*   *   *

While the vice presidential nominee underwent his clandestine nocturnal examination, the other two members of the Constitution Party triumvirate scoured the nation searching for him. Knowing that Roderick Schilling had highly placed sources, Eddie had taken the liberty of having his private plane wait three hours before flying back to its hangar in Columbus. He wanted to make sure no one knew that he was in New York until it was too late to stop him from donating a kidney.

His suspicions turned out to be correct. A check of the flight plan his pilot filed traced him to New York and then home. Roderick incorrectly surmised that Eddie had flown to New York, spoken with his alleged daughter and then quickly gone home, so the search for Eddie concentrated in Ohio.

For his part Eddie had been smart enough to avoid checking into a hotel. After Dr. Orland examined him and spelled out pre-surgical instructions, Eddie left and spent the night before the surgery at a former teammate's home in Connecticut. If things went the way he had planned, by the time the Constitution Party chairman tracked him down Eddie Blanton would be resting comfortably under anesthesia, minus one kidney.

20

The wheels on the chair rolled quietly across the shiny black and white floor. In this new wing of Manhattan General the blue stripe outlining the corridors led to the intensive care ward that Olivia Sagamore and her daughter Jessica had called home for nearly a month after their respective accidents. The morning shift employees were beginning to report for work as Dr. Orland escorted his patient down the hall. Eddie Blanton sat erect and fully aware of the gift he would soon give. Jessica had been informed of his intentions. Her pre-surgery prep had been performed and she was ready for the life-saving operation.

"Good morning Jessica, I'm Eddie Blanton," he said from the wheelchair as he was wheeled into her room just before 6 a.m.

"Good morning," she said weakly.

"How are you feeling?" '

"They've got me doped up pretty good, but it's nothing a new kidney won't fix."

"I've got one in here with your name on it," he said as he patted his taunt stomach.

"I can't thank you enough."

"Nonsense, it's the least I can do. I'm sorry it took something like this to bring us together."

Blanton gazed pensively at Olivia's motionless form laying in the bed across the room. He hadn't laid eyes on her in almost thirty years but to him she was still the beautiful girl from his youth.

Jessica broke the silence, "It's not your fault. Neither one of us knew the truth."

133

"Well, now that we do, I'd like the chance to get to know my daughter."

"And I'd like to get the chance to get to know my father," she said as she reached her hand out to him.

As the two shared a silent moment, Levi Hamilton walked in and their shared silence became awkward.

"Good morning, Levi," Jessica said attempting to break the tension between the two men.

"Good morning, yourself. Are you ready for your big day?"

"Yes, I am."

"Good. I'll be here with your mother waiting for you."

"Okay."

Levi turned to face the man he felt he had wronged. "Thank you, for coming senator. I apologize for bringing you here this way."

"Forget about it, Levi. You've actually given me something I've always wanted but never had. A daughter."

"I wish I had done it differently, sir."

"If I were in your shoes, I would have done the exact same thing. No election is more important than her life."

"Thank you for understanding."

"I understand completely and I admire you for your commitment to uncovering the truth. Now I'll leave the two of you alone while I finish getting ready for the procedure. See you soon, Jessica."

"Thanks again…," she said, almost imperceptibly calling him Dad as he rolled away.

"Boy, that was awkward," Levi said.

"I'm glad he has no hard feelings, and neither will Mom. I know you're worried, but we're all going to get through this just fine."

"Yes, we are," not totally believing the words he'd just spoken.

"As soon as I'm out of surgery, the nurse will bring the baby in for a visit."

"Olivia and I will be waiting."

"Levi, none of this would have been possible if it weren't for you. You've given me a second chance at life. I will always owe you for that."

"I'm glad I was able to help."

"Hi, Jessica, it's time for us to go for a ride." Dr. Orland said as he entered the room.

"You'll have to excuse me, Levi. I'm going to go and have a baby," Jessica said cheerfully.

"Good luck."

"Bye," she said as her bed rolled out the door toward the surgical center.

Levi sat down next to Olivia and began his vigil. Jessica was taken to surgery, where Dr. Orland performed the caesarian. Under local anesthesia in less than a half-hour she delivered a five-pound, two-ounce baby girl. A little small but perfectly healthy. She and Brad had decided to name the baby Olivia Marie, after her mother and Levi's mother. After being given only a precious few minutes to bond with her baby, Jessica was taken into the adjoining surgical unit for her kidney transplant.

"Okay Jessica, one down, and one to go," Dr. Marklewood said when she was wheeled in.

"I suppose at this point it's too late to back out," she said with a smile, trying to mask the fear running rampant inside, the fear that the transplant wouldn't work.

"Not after we got all dressed up," the doctor said from behind his surgical mask.

"Oh, well, since you've gone to all that trouble, go ahead."

"We've already given you a dosage of anti-rejection drugs and now we're going to put you under. You'll be able to see little Olivia in just a few hours," he said with a wink before the anesthesia closed her eyes.

In less than an hour the surgeon had already removed Eddie Blanton's left kidney. Once given the go ahead from the anesthesiologist, he began the surgery to connect Jessica's new organ. During the first hour of her surgery the doctor connected the kidney's renal artery and vein to her iliac artery and vein. The procedure went smoothly and the new kidney began functioning immediately. Since Jessica's kidneys had sustained severe damage in the automobile accident, they would both be removed. The non-functioning organs were taken out and less than three hours after it began the transplant surgery was over.

Levi waited in the room with Olivia while the surgery took place. The room seemed strangely quiet without the constant whirl of the dialysis machine as Levi read aloud the latest headlines from the New York Times.

Brad quickly adapted to his role as a proud father and came in with a picture of his new pride and joy. As the two men waited together, the physical therapist came in for Olivia's daily exercise routine. She was about to begin when she noticed different levels on the monitors. Dr. Orland was quickly summoned to examine his patient.

He checked her ventilator and examined her briefly.

"Is she alright?" Levi asked.

"Yes, she's breathing above the ventilator," Dr. Orland responded matter of factly.

"What does that mean?" Brad asked.

"Her brain is now sending signals to her body telling it to breathe," the doctor said.

"Does that mean she is going to wake up?" Brad asked.

Levi jumped in, "It's a very good sign. Right, doctor?"

"Yes, it is," the chief of staff answered.

"What is her Glasgow Coma Score?" Levi asked.

"She's now up to nine. Her survival percentage is now up to seventy-six percent."

"Thank God!"

"Levi, continue to encourage her and I'll come back and check on her again. Brad, I was on my way in here to tell you that the kidney is functioning normally and Jessica is in recovery. Dr. Marklewood will be in to give you a full update, but it looks like she is going be fine."

"Thank you doctor," Brad said. "Thank you."

*   *   *

While Levi and Brad waited for the nephrologist to arrive, Eddie Blanton rested in his room. In spite of his best efforts, word of his surgery had been leaked to the media, and he knew it was only a matter of time before he was tracked down. He was fast asleep, still recovering, when the phone rang at 11 a.m.

"You've cost us the election with this stunt!" Roderick Schilling spat out.

"Good morning to you, too," Eddie answered. "You may address me as grandpa."

"If I had known you were this stupid I never would have put you on the ticket!"

"You put me on the ticket because I'm your best hope. You know it, and so do I."

"You *were* our best hope but now you've screwed that up!"

"Don't worry, Roderick. I've been behind before and came back to win the game," Eddie said.

"No matter what you think, this is not a game."

"You're right, Roderick, it's not a game. It's my daughter's life," Eddie said before hanging up and falling back to sleep.

*   *   *

After changing into some fresh scrubs, Dr. Marklewood gave Levi and Brad an update on Jessica. The surgery had gone as planned, and so far she had not rejected the kidney. The next seventy-two hours would be critical but the prognosis for a full recovery was excellent.

As Brad rushed out to join his wife, Levi sank down next to Olivia, now staring at her even more intently, searching for any sign at all that she truly was coming back to him. For the first time in his career, his personal life overstepped his professional drive. If he reported everything he knew and observed about the life-and-death situation, it would be a huge story. But his inside track on the story kept his heart where it belonged. After a few moments, he reluctantly left to return to the studio for his nightly broadcast.

21

Video cameras from local and network television news crews lined the wall and bright light flooded the room normally used for weekly staff meetings. Shutters clicked and still photographers anxiously snapped away, as the former quarterback was guided into the room in his wheelchair and parked behind the bank of microphones and tape recorders eager to record his every word.

"Ladies and gentleman, Senator Blanton has agreed to make a short statement and take a few questions. He is still under medical care, so we must make this appearance brief," Dr. Orland said that afternoon to the zealous reporters gathered in the hospital conference room.

Eddie Blanton, tired from the surgery, and lacked his normal vim and vigor. Sitting wearily, he stared directly into the camera broadcasting the press conference live on television and then read the short speech he had written while lying in his hospital bed.

"As you all know, I recently discovered that I have a daughter. I also found out that she needed a kidney transplant and that I was the only person who could help her. Earlier this morning I underwent surgery to donate a kidney to my daughter. It was my decision to do so, and any responsible parent would have done the same thing. I have been told the transplant was successful and that she is resting comfortably.

This morning, prior to the transplant surgery, my daughter gave birth to a little girl, so today I became a grandfather as well. To those who ask why I decided to donate a kidney, the answer is simple. I did so because it was the right thing to do, and I have no regrets. As far as the race for the White House is concerned - I refuse to quit, even though some members of my own party have advised me to.

To the voters of America I say this: If the fact that I fathered a child out of wedlock offends you, and if the fact that I donated an organ offends you - then vote for someone else. That is your constitutional right as an American citizen, and I can assure you that I support your ability to make that choice. But let me make one thing perfectly clear, Eddie Blanton is the Constitution Party nominee, and I am still a candidate for vice president of the United States of America."

"Senator Blanton can you tell us about your surgery and how you're feeling?" one of the reporters asked when the speech was finished.

"My surgery took less than an hour, and I feel fine."

"Senator how is your new granddaughter?"

"She's fine. She was one month premature, and a little underweight, but she's a Blanton and that means she's one tough cookie."

"Have you seen the baby, sir?"

"I've seen a picture of her, and she's the most beautiful baby in the world."

"Senator Blanton, Harry Collier, ECCN. Do you have any hard feeling against the man who exposed your secret?"

"First, let me correct you. There was no secret. I was not aware that I even had a daughter. Now, to answer your question, no. I spoke with Levi Hamilton earlier today before my surgery and I have no ill feelings toward him at all. In fact, I told him that if I had been in his position, I would have done things the same way."

"What's next for you, Senator?"

"First, I'm going to spend some time getting to know my daughter and granddaughter. Then I'm going to spend a few days recuperating and mending fences back home in Ohio. In a week or so, I'll be back on the campaign trail discussing the issues that are important to this nation."

"Senator Blanton, what do you say to those who doubt that the Constitution Party can win this election?"

Eddie paused and reached deep inside himself, gathering his strength, calling on the reserve that had made him a college and a pro football champion. With a fiery look he stared squarely into the camera and forcefully spoke the words that would be broadcast that day on every local and national newscast across the country.

"Eddie Blanton has come from behind many times to win when no one thought he had a chance. I've done it before, and I'll do it again. Anyone who thinks I'm finished really doesn't know me at all."

"Senator?"

"I'm sorry guys, but the senator needs his rest," Dr. Orland interrupted before wheeling the chair out of the room.

"Thanks, doc, I was feeling a little tired after the third question," he said as they left the room.

"No problem. You looked like you could use a break. Besides, there's someone I'd like you to meet in person."

Careful to keep moving quickly away from the eager eyes that recognized the football hero-turned-politician, Dr. Orland took Eddie up to the fourth floor. He slowed when they reached the neonatal wing and parked the wheelchair in front of a large window.

"One second; I'll be right back," the doctor said.

"Okay."

The physician stepped inside the room and spoke with the nurse on duty. She guided him over to an incubator and pointed to the infant inside. Dr. Orland lifted the baby up and walked back through the door he had entered seconds ago.

"Senator Blanton, this is Olivia Marie. She's your granddaughter," he said as he stepped out of the room with a tiny bundle.

The infant was wrapped in a white cotton blanket with bright pink and blue stripes. She wore a pink cap with a white ball on top. Only thirteen inches long, she weighed less than six pounds.

"Can I hold her?"

"Sure."

Eddie gingerly cradled the bundled baby. It had been decades since anyone had placed a newborn in his arms and he felt a rush of emotions he hadn't felt since he'd held his son many years ago. Holding the precious child tenderly, he kissed her tiny hand and silently thanked God for leading him to the right decision.

*   *   *

While Eddie sat marveling at the sight of his first grandchild, Roderick Schilling and Jeff Burris, still hunkered down in Minnesota, discussed the news conference they had just witnessed.

"He's definitely painted us into a corner," Jeff Burris said.

"I don't know if I agree with that," the sage politician said.

"Come on, Roderick, this paternity thing is something we can't overcome. You've got to convince him to pull out for the good of the party."

"Stop and think for a second," Roderick said as he dropped three more cubes of ice into the potent liquor in his glass. "He never knew the girl existed. As soon as he found out about her condition, he went to her, gave her a kidney and saved her life, without regard to whether he was throwing away his political career."

"So?" Jeff Burris wondered aloud.

"So," Roderick said before taking a drink. "Middle America will lap this up. I've spent my whole life in the Midwest and I know how everyday people think. Trust me, this kidney thing is going to make Blanton more a hero than any of those football championships ever did. Instead of skirting the paternity issue, we're going to embrace it."

"It's insane!" Jeff shouted.

"No!" Roderick commanded. "Listen to me. You're a politician. Survival and self-preservation is your natural instinct."

"Agreed. But…"

"What do you think the average politician would have done in that same position?"

"I don't know."

"He would have denied paternity and let the girl die. But not Eddie, he stood up and did the right thing. He put a woman he'd never met, first."

"I think I see where you're going now."

"Yes, we can make this a good thing. Burris and Blanton, not afraid to stand up for the little guy. The two men who will sacrifice anything to fight for you."

"Roderick, you're a genius," Jeff said with reluctant awe when he finally understood the position he was in. "No wonder you're the party chairman."

"Yes, Jeff you're right. I am a genius. Now let's get that campaign manager of yours on the phone and plot some strategy."

Jeff made a call to Tim Reynolds and explained the new direction their campaign would take. At first Tim was skeptical, but Roderick managed to convince him too, and the three men came up with a new plan of action. They decided that as soon as Eddie was back on his feet, he and Jeff would go on the offensive against the Liberty Party. It was their hope and belief that an aggressive approach was best. Thanks to Eddie Blanton, the trio felt that the Constitution Party now had strong momentum on their side.

22

Shortly after Levi and Brad were updated on Jessica's condition she was brought back into the room, peacefully asleep. Three hours later she woke up and Brad updated her on Olivia's improvement. Jessica was on a morphine IV pump, and at first she thought she was confused from the medication, but Brad assured her that her mother was improving.

"Good afternoon, Jessica," Dr. Marklewood said when he returned, "How are you feeling?"

"I'm a little groggy, but otherwise I feel okay."

"Brad, can you and Levi step out for a second while I examine Jessica?"

"Sure," Brad said as he and Levi stood to leave the room.

"I'm going have you sit up for me and cough," the doctor said when they were alone.

"Is it going to hurt?"

"Just a bit, but I you need to cough so you can keep your lungs clear."

"Okay," she said before coughing.

"Again?" the physician said as he listened through his stethoscope.

"Again?"

"Alright, you can sit back," he said as he adjusted her bed. "From time to time you'll need to cough to avoid fluid buildup."

"Everything okay in there?" Jessica asked.

"Yes, everything is perfect so far. Your surgery went well and the new organ is working. Since your kidneys had sustained trauma, we removed them. Each day we will take a blood sample to measure your serum creatinine level. That shows us how efficient the kidney is in eliminating waste products. After your transplant you were at 100. A level of 120 is normal and we can't let you get above 140. As soon as we are sure that the kidney is functioning well and that your body is not rejecting it, you can go home. It's also very important that we keep your blood pressure within normal limits. Over the next week you will notice that your energy level will increase and you won't sleep as much. Tomorrow we are going to remove your fluid IV and your catheter, and you will have to drink four liters of fluid per day."

"Wow, that sounds like a lot," she said.

"It is, but we want that kidney to adjust to being inside you. There is a natural tendency for the body and new organs to battle each other, so we want to keep the new kidney working as much as possible so that it spends less effort and time fighting back. Your IV pump administers meds on your command. If you feel any discomfort, let me or the nurses know immediately. Okay?"

"Okay."

"The two of you can come back in," he said to Brad and Levi.

"How is she?" Brad asked.

"She's is fine, but I think I know how to make her feel better," Dr. Marklewood said as he opened the door wide.

"Someone wants to say hi to mommy," the nurse said as she handed Jessica her daughter. The room filled with a sense of joy.

"I'll see you in a half-hour," Dr. Marklewood said.

"Thank you, doctor," Brad said.

The next day Jessica's tubes were removed and she began short walks down the hall. The second day after her surgery she began to take her anti-rejection drugs orally. The large

Neoral tablets smelled and tasted awful, but she forced herself to swallow them. The baby was allowed to visit several times a day and Jessica took care to make sure Olivia was aware of her granddaughter.

Just before nightfall, Eddie Blanton came into the room dressed in a navy blue Bill Blass original. Looking more like the politician she had seen on television, and less like the man she now knew as her father and who had given her a kidney. At fifty years old he was in great physical shape and it was easy for Jessica to see why her mother had been attracted to him so many years ago.

As she looked at his face, she noticed for the first time that the two of them had the same nose and cheekbones. She wondered how much more they had in common and felt a twinge of sadness that he was the father she'd never had a chance to know.

"Hi, Jessica," he said. "How are you feeling?"

"I'm fine."

"How about your mother and the baby?"

"Mom is getting stronger, and the baby is perfect."

"That's good. I'm happy for you."

"Eddie - may I call you that? I wouldn't be here right now if it weren't for you, so I don't want to seem ungrateful. But I need to know exactly what happened between you and my mother?"

"Of course you can call me Eddie. I met your mother in the spring of 1969. I'm from New York City and I had a football scholarship to Ohio State. I was home with my parents for spring break and went for a swim at the pool at the Westchester Country Club. Your mother played tennis there and she and I met one day at the club. She was so beautiful, and I fell for her the moment I saw her, so things between us happened very quickly. We kept in touch for a year, but I was away at school in Ohio and she was here on the East Coast. We won the national championship that fall and I went pro the next year."

"Were you in love with her?"

"Yes, at that time I was."

"Why didn't you work harder to stay in contact with her?"

"I was so caught up in trying to make a pro team roster that I neglected everyone and everything else. Once I got drafted by Cleveland, I moved there and rarely visited New York."

"When did you get married?"

"Four years after you were born."

"Did you ever have kids?"

"Yes, I have a son. He's a pediatric resident in Columbus. When you get out of here, I'd like you to meet him."

"I'd love to," she said with a smile.

"What's so funny?"

"Here I am, thirty-four years old, and I just got a little brother."

"Jessica, I'm sorry for all of the years we lost, but I'd like for us to try to get to know each other."

"So would I."

"Give me a call when you mother wakes up," he said as he pulled out a pen and wrote down his cell phone number.

"I will. Here, I have something for you," she said as she gave him an envelope.

He opened the envelope and there were two pictures of Jessica and the baby. Brad had taken them the day before.

"Thank you. I had a chance to hold her for just an instant. She's beautiful."

"Yes she is."

"Well, I'd better go. They are releasing me tonight, and once I'm out of this hospital, maybe the media hounds will leave and you and your mother can have some privacy."

"Have a safe trip."

"I will."

"Thanks for the kidney," she said as she gave him a hug.

"Hey, that's what dads are for," he said as he felt wetness on his cheek. "After we win this election, I'll invite you to the White House."

"Good luck."

"Thanks, I'm going to need it," he said before walking out the door.

"You hear that, Mom? We're going to the White House," Jessica said when he was gone.

As Olivia lay quiet with the ventilator continuing to pump oxygen into her lungs, Jessica wondered if her mother would have been happier married to Eddie Blanton than as the wife of Parker Sagamore. Jessica also thought of how different her life would have been as the daughter of a professional athlete. She was reading to her mother when Brad came in for a visit. He stayed while she fed the baby and together they watched Levi on the evening news. Oddly enough, Eddie Blanton was the lead story.

After work that night Levi came to the hospital to check on Olivia. Promising to return the next morning Levi left after an hour of sitting at Olivia's bedside reading and talking to her. The fact that he seemed to care so much for her mother touched Jessica deeply. Her emotions were on edge since the car accident. After the surgery and baby's birth she'd put up a brave front, but her stress had built to an almost unmanageable level. She sent Brad out for a fresh pitcher of water and when the two women were alone Jessica spoke to her mother.

"Mom, Levi cares for you and he needs you. He told me that a few days ago. You have to hurry up and get better. I'm a little weak since the transplant and I need your help with the baby. Plus, I'm scared, Mom, and I can't talk to Brad about it. Transplanted organs don't last forever, and if this one doesn't work I'll have to go back on the donor list. I might have to spend years waiting for another suitable donor. I'm trying to be tough like you, but I'm not that strong. Mom, you *have* to get out of that bed and help me."

Olivia remained still and silent. The sound of the ventilator was the only response Jessica got to her heartfelt plea.

That next morning, three days after her kidney transplant, Jessica got the lift she needed.

"Levi, we have some wonderful news," Jessica beamed when he arrived.

"It must be good. I haven't seen a smile like that from you in a long time.

"It is," she gushed. "Last night Mom was able to breathe on her own for five hours."

"Really?"

"Yes, Dr. Orland came in to check up on her and told me that her breathing signals are improving. They took her out for a CAT scan and the test indicated no structural damage from her fall, and the best news of all - her EEG showed increased brain activity."

"Well, that certainly *is* good news," he said as he walked over to Olivia's bed.

"Yes, and a few hours ago she opened her eyes for the first time."

"Olivia, I'm right here and I'll be here for you when you wake up," he said softly.

The mood in the room was much brighter as the slim hope that Olivia would recover grew stronger. But the mood suddenly plunged when the results of Jessica's daily blood work came back. Her serum creatinine level was high, a signal that she was rejecting the kidney. She was taken back to surgery where a biopsy was performed on her new kidney.

The biopsy results were back in an hour and showed mild rejection of the new organ. Large doses of steroids were prescribed to prevent the rejection and Jessica was switched from Neoral to Tacrolimus, a newer, more effective drug. Much to her delight, the taste wasn't as bitter.

The new drug brought the rejection under control within two days. Over that time Olivia's condition had improved as well. She drifted in and out of sleep and began to show involuntary hand movements and wiggle her toes. She had completed four, six-hour sessions of breathing without the ventilator in the past three days and her Glasgow Coma Score was upgraded to eleven. Since she had been breathing above the ventilator for almost a week, Dr. Orland started to slowly wean her from the machine.

"How are you two this morning?" Dr. Orland asked when he entered the room.

"We're doing just fine, Dr. Orland," Jessica said, cradling her six-day old child. "Aren't we, baby girl?"

"How are you, Olivia?" he asked as he began her morning exam.

"I noticed her moving her hands, and making sounds last night."

"She's coming along nicely. Last night your mother was off the ventilator for eight hours and, after a rest, I'm going to let her try to breathe on her own for twelve hours. If she can do that and has a restful night; I'm going to take her off the ventilator tomorrow."

"Can you wait until Levi arrives? I want him to be here when you disconnect the machine."

"Of course."

Levi, Brad and Jessica sat anxiously the next morning as the technicians disconnected the tubes. It was a day Levi had known would come all along but, clutching his rosary beads, he muttered a decade of Hail Marys as the ventilator was removed. For a few seconds, which seemed like hours, Olivia lay motionless; then her hands jerked a few times and her chest began rhythmically going up and down. A sigh of relief filled the room as her steady breathing continued. Dr. Orland listened to her chest through his stethoscope and checked her blood pressure.

"Everything's normal and she's breathing on her own. We have monitors set up to let us know if her condition changes and we'll keep a close eye on her," he said after writing down her vitals.

"Way to go, Mom," Jessica said softly.

"Olivia, we're waiting for you. Come back to us," Levi said.

23

Eight days after his release from Manhattan General, Eddie Blanton went back to work. With less than six weeks to go before the election he and Jeff Burris hit the campaign trail hard. After an initial rise in popularity immediately following the convention they were currently trailing in the polls by nine percent. Despite Eddie's noble act in New York, most of the nation still disapproved of his illegitimate child.

Roderick Schilling had decided that a show of unity was best, so the two men traveled together and vigorously campaigned side by side. Touching on themes from the platform developed by the party at the convention and focusing on current issues, the two hungry politicians crisscrossed the nation.

No matter how determined the Constitution Party candidates were to stick to governmental concerns, they were dogged by questions about Jessica. After a week of taking the high road, Eddie Blanton decided it was time to fight fire with fire. Speaking to the media after a fund-raiser in Houston he was badgered about his personal life by a particularly contentious reporter. His response changed the tenor of the campaign.

"Senator Blanton, Jim Sandridge with the Lone Star News Network. Sir, President Greenlee says that the fact that you were not forthcoming about your daughter casts doubt on your character. What do you say to that?"

"I think the President should worry more about our growing trade deficit with the Far East, than my personal life."

"So are you saying that the President is correct in his position?"

"No. I am not saying that."

"Senator, exactly what are you saying? The Liberty Party is obviously making your personal life an issue. The President..." he began before he was interrupted.

"The senator has to board a plane now for..." Campaign Manager Tim Reynolds butted in, but he was in turn interrupted.

"Okay, Greenlee wants to play rough. I can play rough too. When the President was Governor of Michigan, he had an affair with his secretary. His wife was hospitalized twice for depression at a sanitarium in Flint over his adultery." Eddie said.

"Eddie, don't," Tim said in a futile effort to prevent Blanton from saying more.

"No, Tim! I've had enough!" The beleaguered candidate shouted as he pulled himself away from the campaign manager.

"Senator Blanton, do you have a response to the president's accusations?" the reporter queried.

"Mr. High-and-Mighty wants to sling mud. Hey, that's fine with me. I can dish it out as well as I can take it," Eddie said as the fiery nature that had led him to gridiron success began to burn brightly. "His oldest son, Anthony Jr., was arrested twice in 1992, once for drug possession and once for trafficking. Don't take my word for it. Go back and check the police records in Pontiac, Michigan. Oh yeah, one more thing. Ask the President about the large donation his gubernatorial campaign received in 1994 from the Alliance Motor Company. It was a four million dollar check deposited in his reelection fund, two days after he suddenly changed his mind and vetoed legislation that would have prevented the layoff of three thousand workers."

"All Greenlee cares about is big business and big government. He screwed the little guys in his own state and he'll do the same to the rest of this nation if he gets a chance. Don't let me fail to mention his sidekick, Matthew Adams, former Congressman from the great state of Mississippi. It was money from the casino political action committees that financed all three of his campaigns. What a change: big shiny hotels sitting on land that was formerly cotton and soybean fields, and no more migrant workers laboring in the ninety-degree heat for minimum wage. Las Vegas fun in the Mississippi Delta, big-time prize fights and national celebrities coming in to entertain the masses. But how many of those high-paying hotel and casino jobs actually went to Magnolia State residents? New four-lane highways built to get eager gamblers to Tunica and Biloxi - but how many new schools and hospitals for working-class people? And should I mention the increase in bankruptcy, suicide, and crime that came with his home state's newfound prosperity? The next time you see the President and the Vice President, Jim, ask a few questions about those subjects. I think the American public would be very interested in hearing the answers."

Eddie was whisked away and boarded the plane for the next campaign stop, but the fire was lit. Hungry for another scandal to feed on, the media frenzy was ratcheted up another notch. Reporters flocked to criminal archives, websites, financial records, and private sources to verify the charges Eddie had leveled.

Within hours his claims were substantiated and the reports flooded the airwaves. Nightly newscasts rebroadcast Eddie's Texas tirade, followed by point and counterpoint analysis of its validity and value. Voters across the nation weighed in with their opinions and the Liberty Party was suddenly put on the defensive.

While Jeff Burris was flabbergasted and disgusted with Eddie's vicious attacks, the rest of his party's leaders were bursting with pride at the verbal assault. The allegations Eddie had lobbed, though well researched and truthful, were known only by a select few, and Roderick Schilling was one in that number.

He had never disclosed those facts to Eddie and was pleasantly surprised that the vice presidential nominee was able to uncover the dirt on his own. Seeing Eddie fight back, unafraid to deliver lethal blows to his opponents, substantiated Roderick's belief. Win or lose this election, Eddie Blanton was a shoo-in for the presidency in four years.

In the week following the senator's blistering speech, momentum began to swing in the Constitution Party's favor. The next voter opinion polls released by USA Today and ECCN showed the Liberty Party's lead trimmed to seven percent. The underdog's fighting-back approach struck a chord with disenfranchised voters, and a new round of political ads swept the nation touting the prior misdeeds and stumbles of the current administration. The negative slant of the campaign revitalized the Constitution Party, and their momentum grew as Election Day approached.

Eddie Blanton became known as the regular guy's politician, a role Roderick had envisioned for him all along, a throwback to the days when he thrilled the nation with Saturday and Sunday afternoon pigskin heroics and come-from-behind victories. He was painted as the man who had, and would, stand up for what was right, no matter what the cost.

Voters and political pundits lauded him on talk shows, and in newspapers coast-to-coast hundreds of column inches were devoted to his 'fighting for the little guy' approach. Jeff Burris continued his campaign stance as the man who was ready to be president, and the re-energized White House seekers increased their efforts on the campaign trail.

24

For the next two weeks the Constitution Party candidates pounded the campaign trail working to narrow their deficit in the polls. Meanwhile at Manhattan General, Olivia Sagamore's health improved. At first she began to turn her head in response to Jessica's voice - but not to Levi or Brad. Then, six weeks after she arrived via med flight from Miami to Manhattan General, she regained consciousness. Levi had arrived for his daily visit before he went to work and was talking to Olivia. Jessica and Brad were busy with the baby.

"Jessica, is Jennifer Lopez really going to marry that TV weather guy? How crazy is she?" Olivia said in a raspy voice.

With her eyes wide open, she spoke clearly in spite of the nasogastric feeding tube in her nose. Everyone in the room froze, looking at one another to make sure they had all heard the same thing. Olivia lay motionless and Levi Hamilton, a journalist who had interviewed many of the most powerful people in the world, was speechless. Jessica handed the baby to Brad and buzzed for the nurse.

"Mom, can you hear me?"

"Yes, of course I can hear you. I'm right over here, aren't I?"

"Good morning, Mrs. Sagamore," Brad said when Jessica motioned for him to speak.

"Good morning Brad," she said, still staring at the ceiling.

"Olivia, it's me. Levi."

"Hello, Levi. Have we met?"

"Yes, but it was a long time ago," he replied, knowing it was best not to confuse her.

"You buzzed the nurse's station?" the white clad woman asked when she entered the room.

"Yes, please get Dr. Orland. My mother is awake," Jessica said, fighting to contain her excitement that her mother's ordeal was finally over.

Within minutes the hospital chief of staff was in the room and at Olivia's bedside. He examined her and found she was lucid but still weak from her ordeal. She requested and was given a small cup of water, and a half-hour after she awakened from her coma the catheter and feeding tube were removed.

"Good morning, Mrs. Sagamore, I'm Dr. Orland."

"Good morning, doctor."

"We've been waiting for you."

"Waiting for what?"

"For you to wake up."

"Oh really? Why is that?"

"You had an accident on your cruise. You fell and hit your head and you've been out for quite awhile," he said as he slowly adjusted her bed, elevating her head, and keeping the rest of the room out of view.

"Oh, my, I've got to get home. Jessica needs me. She's been in an auto accident and she's going to have a baby."

"I'm fine, Mom," Jessica blurted out.

Dr. Orland turned and placed a finger to his lips. He wanted to see how much short-term memory loss Olivia had suffered and he didn't want to confuse her by giving her too much information too fast. The doctor then motioned for Levi and Brad to leave the room. Relieved that she was finally awake but saddened that they were once again banished to the hallway, the two men filed out. Brad took the baby with him so her cries wouldn't startle Olivia.

"Olivia, tell me what you remember about the last few days?" Dr. Orland said calmly.

"My daughter is pregnant and we had lunch right before I left for Miami. She and my son-in-law gave me a cruise as a gift. He is such a nice young man."

"What else do you remember?" the doctor asked as Jessica nervously bit her lip.

"I remember getting on the ship."

"That's good. Do you know where you are right now?" he asked as she still stared straight ahead.

"No."

"You're at Manhattan General Hospital. You're in intensive care."

"Okay."

"I'm going to examine you, okay?"

"That's fine."

The physician gave her a thorough exam and was pleased with the results. Her blood pressure was normal and her Glasgow Coma Score was up to twelve out of a possible fifteen. She was awake for a few minutes more before fading away again. He checked her eye movement and determined that she was merely asleep.

He instructed everyone to continue to read and talk to her but not force her to remember things. The doctor thought it best to let her short-term memory progress at its own pace, especially when it came to the baby and to Levi. Levi was disappointed but did not give up hope.

The next day Olivia was more responsive and alert. She had lost twenty-four pounds but was in fairly good shape, although she was hyper-sensitive to temperature and had to stay bundled up. Late that evening Jessica and Brad were watching the evening news on ECCN when Olivia spoke again.

"Jessica, I went to prep school with that fellow on the news," she said when she saw the familiar face on the screen.

"Yes, Mom," Jessica said, startled by her mother again. "He seems like a nice guy."

"We were on the yearbook staff together."

"What was he like?"

"He," she began and then went silent as she stared at the television.

Jessica sat up and looked at her mother. Olivia had a confused look on her face. Jessica, fearing the worst, reached for the call button to ring for the nurse, but decided to go to her mother's side instead. For almost six minutes Olivia sat frozen as images from her weeklong adventure in the southern Caribbean raced across her mind. Brad helped Jessica from her bed over to sit beside her mother.

"What's wrong, Mom?" she pleaded.

"I remember," she said.

"What do you remember?" Jessica asked as she held her mother's hand.

"The cruise. That man. Everything. I was coming back early because you had a car accident, but I slipped down a flight of stairs. How are you, Jessica?"

"Look at me Mom, I'm fine."

"What about your kidneys and the baby?"

"Everything is fine, Mom, really," she said, afraid to give her mother too much information too quickly.

"He's a wonderful man, Jessica."

"Yes, Mom, you're right. He's been here twice a day, waiting for you to wake up."

"When will he come back again?"

"I guarantee you he'll be here an hour after that news program is over. He comes by every night to say goodnight to you."

"That's good. I want to, I need to see him."

"I know, Mom. I know everything."

"You know?"

"Yes, I do, and, Stella, I'm glad to have you back," Jessica said as the two reunited Sagamore women hugged and cried.

Olivia told Jessica everything she remembered from the wonderful time she and Levi had enjoyed on the cruise. The details were still coming back to her, but she was sure of what she and Levi had shared and how special it was. Forty-five minutes later Levi walked into the room and Brad and Jessica were smiling. Olivia wanted to surprise him with what she had recalled and thank him for his patience.

"Hi, Jessica, how are you feeling?" Levi asked as he always did.

"I'm fine."

"Hello, Levi," Brad said.

"Man, you look as tired as I feel," Levi answered. "How is Olivia?"

"Go on over there and see for yourself," Jessica said coyly.

Her reply confused Levi but he attributed it to the strain she must be under with all that she and her mother had gone through lately.

"Hi, Olivia," he said softly as he removed his overcoat and took a seat.

"Hello, Levi," she said, staring straight ahead.

"How are you feeling?"

"I'm much better."

"Good," he said as he softly rubbed the back of her hand. "I'm glad to hear that."

"I remember, Levi," she said, looking him in the eye for the first time since her fall.

"Good. What do you remember?"

"Peekskill Academy class of 1966 - you were the valedictorian."

"Yes, that's right," he answered, recalling the moment they'd met on the ship.

"I remember the cruise; the hiking, the golfing, the scuba diving, dancing to The Four Tops - and I remember you."

"You do?"

"I love you, Levi."

"Oh, Olivia," he said, as he clasped her hand and kissed her fingers. "You really are back. I love you, too."

After weeks of waiting for her return Olivia had finally come back to him. Her short-term memory had fully recovered and the two laughed and talked about their days and nights on the cruise. Their conversation was warm and comfortable, just as it had been on the ship, and it warmed Jessica's heart to hear her mother so happy.

"I should go and let you get some sleep," Levi said an hour later.

"I know you have to leave, but I hate seeing you go."

"I promise I'll be back first thing in the morning."

"Jessica told me you've been here twice every day."

"Yes."

"Thank you for waiting for me."

"I love you, Olivia. I plan to be at your side for the rest of your life."

"Just like the song says?"

"Yes."

"I believe in you and me," they both said in unison.

Levi kissed Olivia goodnight and gave Jessica a hug before leaving and, just as promised, he returned the next morning. When Levi arrived Dr. Orland was in the room. The doctor finished examining Olivia and opened the curtain separating the two women. He nodded to Jessica and helped her over to her mother's bedside. Olivia was completely free of the fog of her coma and the time had come to bring her up to date on a few things.

"Good morning, Olivia," Levi said.

"Good morning, Levi."

"Mom, we have some things to tell you," she began as she took her mother's hand.

"Go on, I'm listening."

"Mom, I'm not pregnant anymore."

"Oh, my God, what happened?"

"I had the baby, Mom. It's a girl."

"Is she alright?"

"She's perfect. I named her Olivia Marie after you, and after Levi's mother."

"Where is she? I want to see my grandchild," Olivia said eagerly.

"Brad went to get her from the nursery."

"Good, I can't wait to hold her. Why didn't you tell me about her sooner?"

"I recommended waiting until you were stronger. I didn't want to overwhelm you," Dr. Orland cut in.

"Well, under the circumstances, I guess you made the right call," Olivia answered.

"But that's not, all Mom."

"Go on."

"I had a kidney transplant two weeks ago."

"How did you find a donor so soon?"

"Levi helped me."

"Thank you, Levi, that was so sweet of you," she said as she looked warmly in his direction.

"It was the least I could do," he replied as he bit his lip.

"Mom, I need to tell you who the donor was."

"Sure, who was it?"

Olivia had never told Jessica about her father and the news that he was the donor was bound to create some friction. Levi dropped his head, knowing that while his actions had saved Jessica's life, they would now bring Olivia's private shame to light. Although he had acted for a good reason he knew he had betrayed her and he feared her response. Dr. Orland stood ready to move in if necessary.

"Senator Eddie Blanton donated the kidney that I needed."

Everyone in the room stood silent. As Levi slowly lifted his head and his eyes met hers, he saw the pain etched on her face. More humiliated than angry, she buried her face in her hands as if to block out the world and sobbed.

Dr. Orland motioned for everyone to stay put. This was Olivia's first emotional setback since the coma and he wanted to see how she worked her way through the difficult situation. It was difficult for Jessica and Levi to see Olivia in agony, but they followed the doctor's orders.

"How did you know about him?" she said through her sobs.

"I found him," Levi said quietly.

"But I never told you his name."

"I figured it out on my own."

Olivia's tone changed from sorrow to anger. "Why would you do such a thing? I came back here to be her donor. Why couldn't you just leave well enough alone?" she said.

"Yes, I know, but…" he said before she cut him off.

"But you were just trying to get the story. Weren't you? You TV people - anything for ratings. No matter the collateral damage to families!"

Jessica interrupted, "Mom, he had no choice."

"He had a choice," Olivia said. He could have respected my privacy. He had no right to dig into my past. I was on my way here to help you."

Furious, she glared at Levi with eyes seething from betrayal. It was a look that told him he had broken her heart. He knew that once she had a little time to calm down, they'd be able to talk, but he didn't want upset her further. Saying nothing, he quietly left the room and decided to start his workday early.

"Mrs. Sagamore, surgery would not have been an option until today at the earliest. We have no way of knowing if Jessica and the baby would have made it this long. Senator Blanton saved your daughter's life," Dr. Orland said calmly.

Jessica jumped in, "Mom, no one is judging you. Levi didn't mean to hurt you. His only motivation was to help me. His actions persuaded Eddie Blanton to come here."

"He was here?"

"Yes, Mom, I met him. He is a very nice man."

"You talked to him?"

"He told me about how the two of you met and everything that happened."

"Jessica, I'm so sorry you had to find out about him this way. What must you think of me now?"

"I think that I have the greatest mother in the world. She spent decades carrying the burden of guilt over a love affair gone bad that led to a loveless marriage. Just when she meets a man who loves her and is prepared to spend the rest of his life making her happy, she falls into a coma. While she's unconscious, this man puts his career on the line to save her daughter's life. Then she wakes up with a healthy daughter, a new granddaughter, and the man who truly loves her is still by her side. Only a great woman could survive all that - and that's what you are to me."

"Do you really mean that?"

"Of course I do, Mom. The way I feel about you hasn't changed. None of us thinks any less of you. We love you more now, because we got you back when we could have lost you for good. Please don't be angry with Levi. He wanted to make sure the baby and I were around when you woke up."

"I never wanted you to know about Eddie. I promised Parker I would never tell you and that I would never take you away from him."

"It's okay, Mom. I won't forget Dad, and I don't blame you."

"Oh, Jessica..."

"Can we come in now?" Brad asked as he poked his head trough the door.

"By all means, get in here with that baby," Olivia said.

Her mood brightened immediately when she saw her grandchild for the first time. Tears streamed down her face when Brad placed the baby in her arms. Following Levi's lead, Dr. Orland and Brad left the three Sagamore women to bond.

For the rest of the day Olivia cradled her grandchild and fawned over her, only letting go of the child long enough to complain about the hospital food at lunch and dinner. At the end of his workday, Levi Hamilton hailed a taxi to take his customary nocturnal trip to Manhattan General.

"Good evening, Jessica, how are you," he said.

"I'm fine, and so is Mom. She's waiting for you," she said giving him a thumbs-up signal.

"Good evening, Olivia. These are for you," he said as he placed the flowers he'd purchased as a peace offering, on the bedside table.

"Levi, I'm sorry about earlier today. I was way out of line."

"No, I should have respected your privacy. I promise it will never happen again. I just wanted your daughter and grandchild to be healthy and happy when you woke up."

"I know Levi, you did it because you love me."

"Yes, with all my heart, I do."

"That's good, because I feel the same way."

"I know."

"So do you forgive me for lashing out at you?"

"Yes, I do. In fact, I have something else for you."

"What is it?"

"Well, I know you're on a soft-food diet, so I got you something special."

"What is it?"

"You have to close your eyes first."

"What?"

"Come on, I promise you'll like it."

"Okay."

"No peeking, now."

Levi had taken the liberty of stopping by Millennium, one of Olivia's favorite dinner spots, to pick up her favorite meal. He opened the box and pulled out a styrofoam container and a swan-shaped package of aluminum foil, setting them on the tray in front of her. The room filled with the delicious aroma of fresh Maine lobster and a piping hot baked potato. Levi smeared the butter and extra sour cream over the potato for her, the way she liked it.

"Okay, you can open your eyes."

"Levi, you shouldn't have!"

"Hey, this is an excellent hospital and they've taken great care of you but let's face the truth. The food is less than gourmet quality. Now, you go on and eat. Remember to take small bites," he said as he kissed her on the forehead."

"Okay."

"Jessica, I have some for you as well," he said as he walked across the room careful not to wake Brad who, as usual, was asleep.

"Thank you, Levi. I'm glad Dr. Orland is not here. He only allows us to eat bland food," Jessica said.

"Well, I won't tell him about tonight if you don't."

The two women enjoyed their late-night treat and after the lobster, Levi surprised them with tiramisu. When Olivia and Jessica were done, they gave him some good news. The entire Sagamore clan was scheduled to be released from the hospital the next day.

25

The Liberty Party fought hard to negate the allegations fired off by Eddie Blanton, but their denials rang hollow in the face of concrete evidence unearthed by zealous journalists eager to uncover more dirt. Mixing joint and individual appearances, Jeff Burris and Eddie Blanton canvassed the nation pounding away at the incumbents. The harder they worked, the tighter the race became. As the election drew near, the polls showed the two parties separated by only two percent.

Experts predicted that the race for the presidency would be closer than the 2000 Bush/Gore race, making it the closest in history. Sixty-percent of registered voters would likely cast ballots, making it the largest voter turnout since the 1992 Clinton/Bush campaign.

"Thank you, Milwaukee, for such a warm welcome," Jeff Burris said when he stepped behind the podium at the Columbus Day rally.

"We only have three weeks to go until election day, and Senator Blanton and I want to thank you in advance for your support. As he and I have traveled across this great nation, we have listened to your concerns and learned more about the issues that voters across America really care about. Now we want to take what we've learned to Washington and go to work for you. It is obvious that the current administration is out of touch with our country. President Greenlee's administration had forecast a drop in the jobless rate. However, earlier this morning the Labor Department announced that the nation's unemployment rate is six point four percent, the highest it's been since August of 1994. If that's not enough bad news, the trade deficit is still high, crime is running rampant in our cities, interest rates are high, and consumer confidence is low," he continued.

Jessica was watching live coverage of the speech on ECCN as Olivia sat cradling her grandchild. Dressed and ready to leave the hospital, they waited for Dr. Orland to arrive. Jessica muted the television when he entered the room minutes later. He issued final instructions to the two women and gave them the dates and times for their respective appointments for followup care.

"Okay, ladies, as much as I have enjoyed your company, your stay here is over. If you'll just sign these papers, you are free to go," he said as he took out his pen.

"I'm going to miss you, doctor, and I'll never be able to thank you enough for what you've done for Mom and me, but I can't say that I'm sad about leaving."

"Your good health is all the thanks I need and, trust me, no one is ever sad about leaving this place."

"Your chariots await," Levi said as he and Brad breezed in with two wheelchairs.

Almost two months after they had arrived separately at the hospital, Jessica and Olivia departed together. Levi had arranged a limousine for the trip, and within an hour they were safely home at the Westchester County mansion Olivia's grandfather had built with his own two hands.

26

"It is now nine o'clock and the polls are closing up and down the eastern seaboard and across the southern states. ECCN has eleven correspondents strategically positioned around the nation to provide you with comprehensive coverage. As we all learned four years ago it's the electoral vote, not the popular vote, that is crucial for choosing a new president, and the electoral tally will be our focus tonight," Levi Hamilton said from behind the news desk, three weeks after Olivia and Jessica had been released from medical care.

Although early returns showed the incumbents leading the race, both parties expected a long night of anxiously waiting for final vote totals. Exit polling of voters confirmed that it would be a very close race and after trailing early, the Constitution Party quickly closed the gap once returns from the southern states began to filter in.

"We are ready to update the number of votes for the two candidates. ECCN declares Florida, Pennsylvania, Illinois, Indiana and Michigan for the Liberty Party. With twenty five percent of precincts reporting, the Liberty Party ticket has a lead of over two hundred thousand popular votes. That gives President Greenlee one hundred of the two hundred and seventy electoral votes he needs for re-election," Levi said to the two political pundits sitting next to him.

Former Greenlee campaign adviser Jocelyn Watts spoke first. "This is great news for the President. Obviously carrying his home state of Michigan is no big surprise, but Pennsylvania is a huge plus. He needs to build a sizeable lead early since he has to concede California. If he wins New York, maybe the race is over"

"Jeff Burris may be the governor but President Greenlee ran well out west four years ago, and I'm not so sure he can't win California," said ECCN Senior Political Analyst Howard Silas. "But I agree with you: the state he needs to be concerned about is New York. Those thirty-three votes can negate Burris' California advantage."

"With that said, ECCN is now ready to declare New York for the Constitution Party. Combined with the southern bloc of Tennessee, Arkansas, Mississippi, Alabama, Georgia and the Carolinas, this gives Jeff Burris one hundred and one votes," Levi said.

"Those Southeast results were expected, since that is a Constitution Party stronghold. Although I'm a little surprised that they lost Florida," Jocelyn Watts said.

"You can attribute that to the backlash against Governor Ward Cargellon. He is in deep trouble down there, and tonight his fiscal difficulties hurt the party. I doubt very seriously if he gets re-elected when this term is over," Howard Silas said.

"Additionally, the Constitution Party has taken a slim lead in the popular vote with a thirty thousand vote advantage," Levi said. "Now we're going to step away from the race for the White House and update you on some gubernatorial elections across the nation. Our first stop will be the hotly contested race in Ohio where Clayton O'Neal is attempting to become the state's first African American Governor. For an update on that situation let's go to Natalie Jamison."

After receiving updates on six gubernatorial races across the nation, Levi steered the coverage back to the presidential race.

"ECCN now declares Kentucky and West Virginia for the Burris/Blanton ticket, another thirteen electoral votes. The

Constitution Party has now taken its popular vote gap to just over one hundred sixty thousand votes," Levi added fifteen minutes later.

"The three big prizes still left on the board are; Ohio with twenty-one votes, Texas with thirty-two, and, of course, California with fifty-four votes," Jocelyn said.

"If either party can sweep those two states, then it's look out White House, here they come," Howard said.

"Okay, then, give me your predictions for those three states?" Levi asked.

"I think Burris takes Ohio, Greenlee takes Texas, and California is up for grabs," Jocelyn said.

"No way," Howard said. "Greenlee takes Texas. Eddie Blanton delivers Ohio, and Burris takes his home state. And come January we're inaugurating a new president."

The polls in California would not close for another hour, and it was likely that those results would decide the winner. Texas went to the incumbent and Eddie Blanton's football connections delivered Ohio to his party. By the time the polls closed out west, President Greenlee had the lead with two hundred and thirty-four electoral votes and held on to a slim lead of eight votes.

Moments after the polls closed in California, ECCN was the first network to declare a victor. On the strength of his home state, Jeff Burris, Governor of California, unseated the incumbent and was elected President of the United States of America. Eddie Blanton, the perennial underdog, had won once again.

A month after the election, on a clear, cold December Saturday afternoon, Olivia Cavillian Sagamore wed Levi Hamilton in a grand ceremony at St. Patrick's Cathedral in New York City. Vice President Elect Eddie Blanton attended the ceremony. A photo of him holding his granddaughter while dancing with his daughter, Jessica, at the reception, made the cover of People magazine.

Dear Reader:

The original title for this book was Seventeen Days. The basic premise was for two old high school friends to reunite on a cruise. In a seventeen day stretch, they would meet, fall in love, and she would die. But over the course of writing and editing this story, I met, fell in love with, and married a wonderful woman. She has totally changed my world and I can't imagine living without her, so I decided to keep Olivia Sagamore and Levi Hamilton together as well. Besides, in my first three mysteries I've whacked over a dozen people and I wanted to see if I could write a mystery where no one dies. As always thanks for taking the time to read the book and I'll see you on TV.

Chris